THE BOOK OF BEASTS

Journey through time
with Matt and Emily Calder:

Hollow Earth
Hollow Earth: *Bone Quill*

HOLLOW EARTH

THE BOOK OF BEASTS

JOHN BARROWMAN &
CAROLE E. BARROWMAN

Aladdin   New York   London   Toronto   Sydney   New Delhi

ALADDIN

An imprint of Simon & Schuster Children's Publishing Division
1230 Avenue of the Americas, New York, New York 10020
This Aladdin hardcover edition October 2015
Text copyright © 2014 by John Barrowman and Carole E. Barrowman
Jacket illustration copyright © 2015 by Nigel Quarless
Interior illustrations copyright © 2012 by Buster Books
Interior illustrations by Andrew Pindar
Originally published in 2014 in Great Britain by Head of Zeus Ltd.

For information about special discounts for bulk purchases, please contact Simon & Schuster
Special Sales at 1-866-506-1949 or business@simonandschuster.com.
The Simon & Schuster Speakers Bureau can bring authors to your live event.
For more information or to book an event contact the Simon & Schuster Speakers Bureau
at 1-866-248-3049 or visit our website at www.simonspeakers.com.
Jacket designed by Jessica Handelman
Interior designed by Mike Rosamilia
The text of this book was set in Goudy Old Style.
Manufactured in the United States of America 0915 FFG
2 4 6 8 10 9 7 5 3 1
Library of Congress Cataloging-in-Publication Data
Barrowman, John, 1968– author.
The Book of Beasts / by John and Carole E. Barrowman. — First Aladdin hardcover edition.
p. cm. — (Hollow Earth ; [3])
Summary: Possessing extraordinary powers, including the ability to bring artwork to life,
twelve-year-old twin Matt Calder must find a way to return from the Middle Ages
and prevent his father from taking control of the beasts of Hollow Earth.
[1. Magic—Fiction. 2. Art—Fiction. 3. Twins—Fiction. 4. Brothers and sisters—Fiction.
5. Time travel—Fiction.] I. Barrowman, Carole E., author. II. Title.
PZ7.B275679Bo 2015
[Fic]—dc23
2014030204
ISBN 978-1-4814-4230-5 (hc)
ISBN 978-1-4814-4232-9 (eBook)

To Jim Higgins
for taking a chance on a local writer
and
to Finnegan Mathieson Murray,
welcome to this crazy, wonderful family

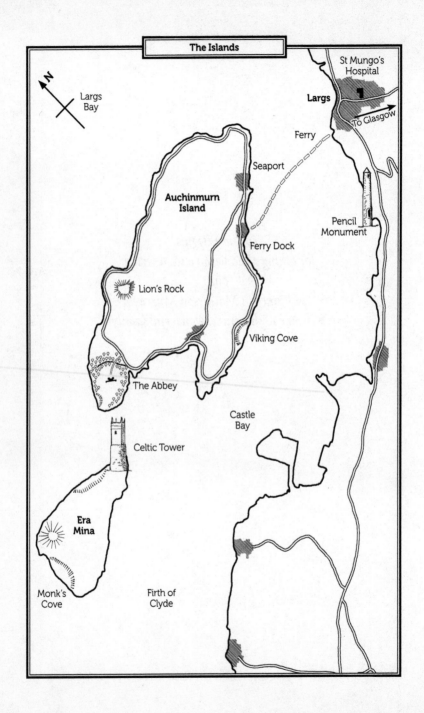

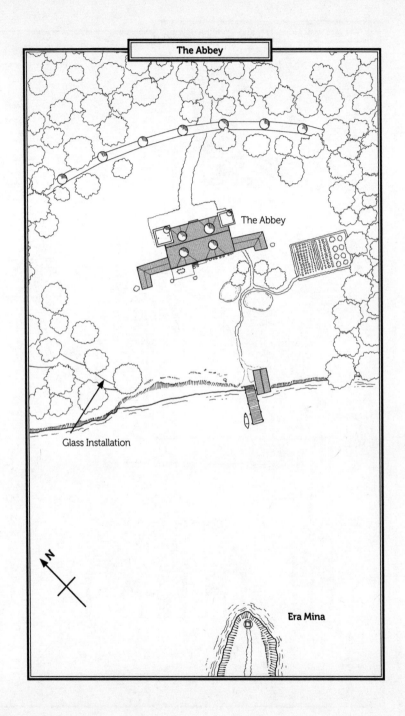

The Abbey

Glass Installation

Era Mina

PART ONE

Be careful when you fight the monsters, lest you become one.

—FRIEDRICH NIETZSCHE

ONE

Duncan Fox stood on the craggy hillside of Era Mina, squinting against the late-summer sun that drenched the Isles of Bute and Arran in a golden light. He was waiting for his canvas to dry, but his mind was elsewhere. With his hands deep in the pockets of his tweed field jacket, he was thinking about the visitors he had recently received: Sandie Calder and her children, Emily and Matt.

My family, Duncan thought. *From a future I can hardly imagine.*

He wondered if the recent hauntings he had been experiencing were a consequence of their visit.

The first time he had seen the strange figure, Duncan thought what he was seeing was a lucid dream: a state where he had a solid awareness of his surroundings while he slept. He had experienced such dreams before, but never so dramatically.

One week ago, he had sat up in bed, drenched in sweat, a vague feeling of dread raising the hair on the back of his neck. A gust of wind from Largs Bay swept open the curtains, carrying with it the smell of the seaside—salty kippers, crushed shells, briny sand. Reaching for the pitcher of water next to his bed, Duncan poured himself a glass, then promptly spilled it onto the floor. A shadowy figure had stepped out from the corner next to his wardrobe.

He hurriedly lit his oil lamp and held it above his head as the figure morphed from a ghostly presence to a fully fleshed man dressed in a brocade robe with a thick collar plate woven in shimmering golden threads—a druid, magnificent and majestic. The druid's robes were white with a silver helix embroidered on the breast. The vision wore a crown of twisted antlers, a fur cloak draped from iron clasps at his shoulders. His left hand gripped a scepter cut from a length of knotty white pine with a carved peryton perched on its tip, and there was a sword with a peryton at its hilt in his right hand. Duncan could see him as clearly as he could see the portrait of his own grandfather hanging on the wall behind him.

The figure had remained at the foot of the bed until the light of morning banished him, leaving Fox with a vague feeling of unfinished business.

This had continued for six nights. Between nights four and five, Fox had called for his carriage and ridden alone on the coast road to Ayr to seek advice from one of the oldest Guardians in Scotland.

Frances MacDonald's fingers were gnarled from arthritis, but her eyes were bright and her intellect keen as Duncan carefully described his vision. She pointed to the first volume of *The History of Religion and the Decline of Magic in Scotland*.

"That was once required reading for our kind," she said. "You'd do well to read it now if you're looking for answers. Lift it down for me."

Duncan took the volume from the shelf and set the book on the table. Then he waited as her fingers slowly turned the thick pages, his hands folded behind his back, patient and respectful of her age.

"Is this who's comin' to ye in the dark?" she asked, stepping away from the table to reveal a full-page facsimile from an illustrated manuscript.

Duncan stared at the image. The white robe, the fur cloak, the wooden scepter with its carved peryton. Every detail, from the twisted crown to the silver helix on the figure's breast, was identical to the figure who had been appearing at the foot of his bed.

"That's him!" he said in astonishment. "Who is he?"

"He is Albion. The Guardian of the Beasts in Hollow Earth."

The old woman returned to her chair next to the cottage's bay window and lifted her knitting onto her lap. Despite her twisted fingers, her knitting needles clacked with unnatural speed.

"Hollow Earth?" Duncan repeated.

"Aye." She nodded. "Hollow Earth. Many think the place a mere story told to children. But it is as real as this room.

"Albion is the first of our kind. He was called to these islands in a dream. Some believe it was the twin perytons, the black and the white, that called him to found the monastery on Auchinmurn as a safe haven for Animare and Guardians alike."

Fox perched on the edge of a wooden chair, listening intently. The old woman set her needles on her lap and continued.

"The beasts who now live only in our stories, our myths and fables, once lived and breathed in Albion's world. Griffins, basilisks, selkies, and more. But when magic was no longer trusted and the world had new ways of explaining matters, there was no safe place for creatures such as these. It was Albion who began the task of sealing the beasts away. He started *The Book of Beasts*, indexing and categorizing as he locked them far beneath the islands in the place we call Hollow Earth."

"Have you ever heard of Albion manifesting himself in dreams in this way?" Duncan asked. "Outside Hollow Earth?"

The old woman's eyes were starting to droop. Outside her window a farmer on his milk cart trundled along the cobbled street.

"I have heard it said that Albion is the one from whom we are all descended," she mumbled. "Which makes the Council laws that keep us apart, when we're all from the same stock, as daft as dust."

Her chin dropped to her chest. Duncan realized she was snoring.

Quietly he lifted his overcoat from the back of the kitchen chair, pulled a bill from his money clip, and set it under the marmalade jar at the center of the table. As he lifted the latch on the door, the old woman suddenly roused.

"Mr. Fox," she said. "If yer visitor is Albion, then you and your sons and daughters may be in danger."

Duncan smiled in surprise. "Mrs. MacDonald, I am a . . ."

. . . *confirmed bachelor.*

He stopped himself from finishing the sentence.

The old woman was referring to Sandie and the twins.

TWO

Duncan Fox took to sitting up and waiting for Albion to appear. The same thing happened for the next two nights. A little after midnight, there would be the elongated figure gliding out of the corner of the room, slipping to the foot of the bed. Albion never came closer than the foot of the bed. He never did anything more than raise his scepter above his head.

On the seventh night, everything changed.

That night, Albion appeared after midnight as usual. But instead of floating above the Oriental rug in the bedroom with the portrait of Fox's grandfather visible behind him, Albion stood before an entirely different backdrop. A rocky opening, dark and shimmering. Fox recognized it at once. It was a cave tucked into the northwest hillside of Era Mina: the small island opposite the main isle of Auchinmurn.

On that seventh night Fox shifted cautiously to the end of his bed, wary of disturbing the apparition but intent on examining the cave.

The cave mouth expanded, in an ever-widening gyre, hitting Fox with a blast of fetid air. Albion raised his scepter, holding it out toward him.

Not knowing what else to do, Duncan grasped it.

At once he was lifted off his bed. All of a sudden, the pursing mouth of the cave had become a twisting tunnel of spiraling colors and light; a maelstrom of yellows, grays, and blacks. At first it was impossible for Duncan to tell if he was falling or rising, tumbling forward or flipping back. He was weightless, and yet there was pressure pushing on all sides of his body. His hand gripped the wooden scepter more tightly, sensing that somehow it was controlling his descent.

And then he heard the beasts.

Howls. Bellows. Cries. All of them thunderous, all of them monstrous. A scaly claw burst through the swirling colors, tearing the sleeve of his pajamas. A hundred harpies swarmed like bats at his feet, snapping their needle teeth at his bare toes.

Duncan kicked and batted them away in terror. Albion's scepter flew from his nerveless hand. In that instant, he landed face-first on his bed with a thump.

He had rolled over quickly, gasping and scrambling to his feet. The morning sun was streaming in through the parted curtains. Albion had gone.

The sun was warm on Duncan's face now. He studied his painting again, then looked back at his subject: the old smugglers' cave. It was the place that Albion had shown him. He was sure of it. Sandie Calder and her children were in danger from this place. Somehow. At some time.

THREE

AUCHINMURN ISLE
WEST COAST OF SCOTLAND
THE MIDDLE AGES

High up on the burned and blackened hillside, an elderly woman in a bright orange safety vest pulled her hands from the cold earth and watched the rising wave stretch itself over the bay. Jeannie Anderson had done what she could to protect the island and its secrets her entire life, as was her birthright, her sacred duty. This wave was so powerful that it would destroy most of the island, but it had to be done. *The Book of Beasts* could not fall into the wrong hands. Ever.

Jeannie sat back on her heels, prepared for her own death.

She suddenly tensed in alarm. Something was wrong.

Someone was out of time.

* * *

The monstrous wave blotted out the sun.

From settlements up and down the Scottish coast, men, women, and children fled to higher ground. A few fell to their knees, howling to the heavens for mercy. Deer darted deeper into the forest; sheep cowered under hedgerows. Cormorants flew to crannies on the cliffs, leaving a flock of herring gulls hovering above the shore, circling, cawing, waiting to pick flesh from the dead.

Carik, a pale Norse girl with elfin features and lively blue eyes, stood with Matt Calder and Solon, an apprentice Animare at the monastery. Carik's blue eyes were wide.

"Matt of Calder, is your dark magic controlling the sea?"

Watching the wave rise above them, Matt shook his head. "Someone else is doing this." *Someone more powerful than me*, he thought. "And I'm going to find out who."

Without warning, he took off down the hillside, heading back to the beach.

"Matt, stop!" yelled Solon. "You may come from a place I don't understand, but I know this. That wave will kill us all!"

Unsheathing his sword from his leather belt, the young monk charged after Matt. But Carik, who had separated the two boys in a fight earlier that day, stepped in front of him with her hand on his chest.

"Let him go. We owe him no fealty. Let him fight his own battle."

Solon shook her off. "This isn't only his battle. I owe my allegiance to these monks. These islands are my home."

The wave stretched closer, arching over the tall band of pine trees bordering the shoreline, drenching the island in salty brine. There was no time left. Carik and Solon threw themselves under a lip of the hillside, bracing themselves for the impact.

The wave shivered like a living thing, but didn't fall.

"What sorcery is holding it?" asked Carik, peering out in astonishment.

"I don't know, but we need to get to higher ground." Solon seized his pack and grabbed Carik's arm, pulling her from under the rock and up the hillside, through the trees toward the abandoned cottage where they'd been hiding since the attack on the abbey. "If Matt's father is the dark monk terrorizing my islands, Matt will need our help to stop him. We can't help anyone if the sea swallows us first."

"But he doesn't want our help!"

"I don't care what he wants," said Solon, blinking against the swelling under his eye that Matt had inflicted in their earlier fight. "I will not have any more blood on my hands."

A brilliant beam of light breached the darkening sky, cutting through the curling, shivering crown of the wave. Carik shielded her eyes as the white peryton swooped across the sky toward them.

The size of ten stallions, the magical beast was an awe-inspiring sight as its huge hooves touched the ground in the clearing before them. With its wings folded against its powerful haunches, it galloped to a stop in the middle of a copse of trees. Its presence overwhelmed the small space. Steam rose from its flaring nostrils, and its silvery hide glistened with droplets from the wave now hanging like a heavy cape over the trees.

Stamping its front hooves impatiently, the peryton knelt before Solon. Not for the first time, nor for the last, Solon wondered at the ways that this ancient beast was connected to him and to the islands. Ways that he might never fully understand.

He climbed onto the beast's back, adjusting his sword before helping Carik up behind him. The peryton took four great galloping strides and lifted into the air. Slipping backward, Carik scrambled in panic to steady herself as the peryton rose over the wave.

Solon!

Clear as a bell, Solon heard Carik in his head. Her Guardian abilities had disturbed him at first, but he now found himself welcoming them. He grabbed the belt of her tunic, hauling her close to him. As she put her arms around his waist, he felt her heart drumming against his back. For a brief moment Solon savored the tingling warmth.

A freezing, wet wind buffeted them as they rose into the sky. Carik tucked herself against him. Solon leaned forward, tightening his grip on the beast's tines, letting his thoughts of saving Matt and the monks drift through his fingers into the skein of fur coating the antlers, deeper and deeper until Solon knew that the peryton understood what must be done.

The peryton soared higher. Below them the dark wave looked like the hungry maw of a sea monster.

FOUR

The curtains were rippling in a light breeze. Too chilled to get out of bed and shut the window, Em Calder rolled onto her side under her duvet, hoping to snag a sweatshirt from the pile of clothes on the floor. Reaching out, she touched a gloved hand.

"Aaargh!"

Em screamed and shot up in bed, fumbling to find the switch on her beside lamp. Then she realized she didn't need it. The center of her room was already awash in a pale yellow light.

A druid-like figure wearing a crown of knotted antlers stood next to Em's bed. Except—he wasn't next to her bed, exactly. He was standing on the rocky ledge of a cliff instead of her bedroom floor. Tendrils of fog like dry ice swirled around the figure's leather-stockinged feet, chilling the room.

Em had always been a lucid dreamer, often waking in the middle of the night with her dreams surrounding her. Her bedroom would fill with the wispy trails of storybook characters darting to and fro—grinning cats, young knights, and wizards. But some nights she'd wake to horrible things. Swooping dragons with snakes' eyes hovering above her. Demons lurking in the shadows, monsters, and madmen. When they crowded her room, their presence was so strong, so fully animated, that they would bring Em's mum, Sandie, rushing in, waving madly, exploding them into a million points of white light.

She had learned to quiet many of her fears and dreams since coming to the abbey. But when she and her mother had returned from the Middle Ages without Matt, all the control she had gained—asleep and awake—had been crushed under the weight of her longing for her brother.

Em didn't think things could get any worse, especially after learning from her grandfather that the terrible monk in the purple cloak who had stood on that burning hillside in the Middle Ages had been her own father, unbound from his painted prison by Matt himself.

In the days following these revelations, Em had moped round the abbey compound, restless and disconnected. She and Matt had never been separated from each other for any significant length of time, and Em kept imagining she could hear him sneaking up behind her or sitting next to her at meals. But he was never there. He was a phantom presence, a lost limb, haunting her.

During those first dark days, the other adults at the abbey had insisted Em stay inside to avoid any serious manifestations of her fears. One day, when she had wandered down to the beach from the kitchen, Jeannie's rosebushes had burst from the soil one after the other, sprouted feet, and trotted behind Em like ducklings, their buds opening and closing in unison. It had taken hours to catch them all, and even yesterday Em was convinced she'd spotted one of the animated roses grinning at her from behind a tree.

Without Matt, there was only one other person who could help her: Zach.

Zach Butler's Guardian abilities connected him to Matt, but his connection to Em was much deeper. Deaf since birth, Zach communicated through signing and lipreading. He also connected with Em telepathically. He looked like a younger version of his dad, Simon—tall and fit, with a soccer player's athleticism.

Zach! Em shouted in her head. *Get in here. Quick.*

She stared at the robed figure, who stared back. *I'm cracking up*, she thought.

Em fished frantically under her pillows for her comic. She had been working on the piece about a warrior princess for several days, drawing and shading as a way of keeping her mind away from thoughts of Matt. She had fallen asleep last night revising several panels. Had she drawn this guy as some kind of secondary character? She didn't recognize him. She flipped the pages. He wasn't in her comic book.

Rolling up the comic, Em hurled them at the figure. Instead of exploding into slivers of light and fragments of color as most of Em's lucid dreams usually did, the figure shifted slightly to his left. The comic fluttered to the floor.

Em scrambled back against her headboard. "Seriously! Who are you?"

The figure wore a long white wool robe with a wide collar that was stitched in golden threads like a tapestry. At the center of the heavy robes was a swirling silver helix. The more Em stared, the more the helix appeared to pulse.

Behind the figure Em noticed an impression in the rock face that shimmered and stretched up into her bedroom ceiling. It was as if the figure had stepped out of the rock itself. The rock was shot through with silver veins, and looked to Em a lot like the cliffs of Era Mina, the small island that faced the abbey across a short strip of water.

A fur cloak hung from iron clasps in the shape of a peryton at his shoulders, and in his right hand, he gripped a sword with a similar beast on its hilt. His limbs were long and lithe, and with his chiseled jawline and his wavy dark hair curling onto his shoulders, he reminded Em of a younger version of her ancestor Duncan Fox. Or an older version of Matt.

The figure opened its mouth, releasing a rush of fetid air. Gagging, Em covered her nose with her pillow. It wasn't just his breath that reeked. His entire body smelled of filth, sweat, and wet fur. He smelled feral. Like a wild animal.

Zach! Wake up!

The figure cocked his head, startling Em. Had he heard her?
He had dodged the comic book. He was aware of her presence.
This was no lucid dream. This was something else entirely.

FIVE

Matt scrambled through the tangled briar beneath the hanging wave. He had to reach the shore before the monstrous wall of water crashed down and obliterated the island. If his father had created this wave, he had to know.

He thought about drawing, animating something to help him get to the shore faster. But as he dodged and ducked and darted through the drenching spray from the wave and the muddy ground under him, all he could picture were his mother and his sister. Dead, because of him. Killed by his own father, because of him.

He wiped his tears with his sleeve and charged on through the woods. He would stop this wave, somehow. Stop his father from inflicting any more damage on the monks, the monastery, and the future.

Matt barreled out of the trees and hit a wave of flowing mud streaming down the hillside. He fell, landing awkwardly on his backside. Slewing from side to side in the wet brown cascade, he let his momentum carry him under one lashing branch, then another, until he got his footing again. Thunder crashed, sending the white tips of the great wave smashing into the treetops like a thousand angry ghosts and drenching Matt with their salty spray.

In the past days, Matt had been beaten and betrayed, abandoned and humiliated. Under normal circumstances, perhaps one of those things would have been tolerable, but taken together they were simply too much for him to bear. Matt was so angry with himself and his world that he thought he might breathe fire. He plowed on through the thick brush. A crooked tree branch whipped in front of his face. He didn't duck in time and it slashed across his cheek, drawing blood. Matt cursed, slowing his clumsy descent enough to wipe the cut with his other sleeve. Glancing up, he glimpsed the white peryton lifting Solon and Carik up into the scudding clouds.

"Stop this madness, Matt! You can't control the sea!" Solon yelled down at him.

Wanna bet?

The gale force of the winds whipped through the trees, assaulting Matt from all sides. A branch cuffed the back of his head; another swatted his back. His chest ached from sprinting down the hill. He swerved to avoid a falling pine branch and, lightheaded, grabbed another tree root to steady himself. At once the ground began to tremble beneath him, sending shock waves of pain up his arm and across his shoulder. Shouting in pain, he let go, tumbling backward into a spindly bush.

Was his father controlling the sea? But how? Malcolm Calder was a Guardian, not an Animare. Guardians couldn't bring drawings to life. A Guardian's expertise lay in empathy, and communication with the Animare they were sworn to protect. Calming them when their fears exploded, stopping their imaginations from creating terrible things. There was nothing calming or empathetic about Malcolm Calder. Matt had already seen how his father had used his powers of mind control for evil, inspiriting the monks of Auchinmurn to do his will, turning them into his zombielike minions, forcing them to murder two of their own—all in order to steal a sacred bone quill that would help unleash the fantastical, dangerous beasts locked away in Hollow Earth.

Matt understood now that jealousy had driven Malcolm to this madness, and hunger for the dual abilities that his children shared. Malcolm had to be behind the wave. Because if it wasn't his father's doing, whose was it?

Losing his footing again, Matt landed flat on his back in the hard sand. The fall punched the air from his lungs. Gulping frantically to catch his breath, he stared up at the burned and blackened swath of hillside where Solon and Carik had last seen Em and his mum alive, before they had apparently burned to death among the trees.

What he saw there made him forget about the wave, the water, his grief, his dad, and his own desperation.

Dressed in an orange safety vest, with her apron underneath, Jeannie, the abbey's housekeeper, stood ankle deep in the muddy earth above the beach, her palms raised to the thundering heavens.

Matt's Guardian senses smashed into his brain like a speeding truck.

The wave had been in Jeannie's control from the start. She had realized he was on the island. Having created the wave, she was holding back the sea to give him a chance to survive. But the effort was destroying her. Matt felt her power weakening, her hold over the water fragmenting, her mind closing in on itself.

A balloon of icy salt water dropped from the wave. When it hit the ground near Matt's head, it exploded. A fist-size blue crab appeared, a gaping mouth snapping angrily where its eyes should have been.

"Jeannie! Let the wave go," Matt screamed.

Matt could sense her collapsing like sand, her control weakening further. He struggled to his feet. The creatures were carpeting the beach now. Matt dodged them when they lunged for his ankles, running toward Jeannie, but there were too many. He tripped, falling flat on his face. The creatures skittered up his legs, along his arms, hundreds of them smothering him beneath their slimy, salty shells, their mouths snapping and sucking at his exposed flesh. They pressed him deeper into the sand. Their pincers tore at his neck and his face. Everything Matt had been trying to keep at bay jabbed at him. Every living thing on these islands, on this coastline, in this time, was going to die. *And it is my fault.*

A crab chewed a chunk of flesh from his ear, and Matt shouted with grief and pain. He tore the crab away, his blood trickling down his neck. "Enough!" he screamed into the sky.

With a massive effort, he wrenched himself free, tossing the creatures from his shoulders, shaking them from his back, brushing them from his arms and his legs. The crabs crunched under his boots, leaving puddles of blue in his wake.

He took the opera glasses he'd hidden in his pocket and looked up at the hillside. He saw immediately that Jeannie's eyes were sliding in and out of focus, and he gasped at the weight of the old housekeeper's love for him. He read her barely moving lips.

"Draw something, son. Or yer gonna drown."

SIX

The druid's piercing black eyes followed Em the way a portrait in a gallery sometimes seems to, but he never moved a limb, never shifted from his place on the rocky ledge. A strange pulsing energy was coming from him, a line of concentration so intense it was as if he held only one emotion, one significant thought, one focus. Em wondered if this was why he wasn't moving. It was taking all his energy to put himself here in her room.

Zach! Wake up!

What was it about teenage boys that they slept through anything? Obviously Zach didn't hear the normal things that woke people—hooting owls, car alarms. But his own Animare, screaming in his head?

Em could hear her grandfather Renard's calm tones in her

mind. *Some Guardians can settle their minds so that they can sleep without hearing or feeling their Animare's presence all the time.*

Whatever the reason, Zach was not responding.

Shivering from the increasing chill in her bedroom, Em flipped through her other sketches. She couldn't find anything even *resembling* this guy.

Hugging her pillow to her chest, she stifled a sob. She'd been missing Matt so intensely that she hadn't been sleeping much or eating well. Maybe her mind was cracking after all. And once it cracked, then there would be nothing anyone could do to save her. Like other Animare throughout history—da Vinci, Gauguin, van Gogh, and so many more—the Council of Guardians would be forced to bind her. She would never be able to draw again.

Suddenly Em felt an overwhelming desire to draw.

She turned to a clean page on her sketch pad and began to outline the apparition, smudging the charcoal with the heel of her hand, darkening the helix shape on her sketch, trying to ignore the rancid smell of him. The more she focused on the drawing, the clearer the figure in the room became, as if her rendering him on paper was giving him more strength. When she finished capturing him, she drew the landscape behind him as quickly and skillfully as she could. As she drew, the glow around him began to get stronger while the room got darker. Em lined and looped and shaded frantically across the paper.

"Can you hear me?" she asked, looking up from her drawing for a beat. "Who are you?"

Em dropped her charcoal. A dark hole had burst open on the rock face behind the figure in a swirling storm of yellows, blacks, and grays. For a fleeting moment, Em felt that she had seen this all before.

Now he was inside her head, projecting a deep resolve for something. A task? A quest? No, it was a warning!

His thoughts were coming to her not as words but as lines of color, strings of yellows, reds, and cobalt blue floating behind her eyes. Em tried desperately to grasp them, to give them shape, but she couldn't. She felt light-headed, her eyes gritty like they were full of sand.

Then the figure lifted his scepter toward Em. Without hesitation, she touched it.

She was plunged into a widening gyre, a sucking hole that had opened at the side of her bed. The force of it pulled Em knee deep before she had enough sense to grab the leg of her bed and hang on for dear life. A stack of books, an empty cereal bowl, a tennis racket, and a wet towel smacked against her as they disappeared into the swirling vortex. The figure stood over her, the end of the scepter spinning above her head.

As her bed lurched toward the hole, Em had a sudden flash of the abbey itself being sucked into the vortex and disappearing forever, leaving nothing but the footprint of its foundations. She tried to scream, but the sound came out as a choking cough.

Her easel lifted off its stilts and flew at her. Instinctively, she lifted her hand to cover her head, and lost her grip on the leg of the bed.

Flapping her arms did nothing to halt Em's momentum. She plummeted into the maelstrom. The deeper she fell, the faster she appeared to drop. Yet when Em looked up, she could still see the edge of her bed, her purple duvet, her sketch pad open on her pillow, the moonlight streaming in through her curtains.

Her ears began to pop; her body felt like someone was pressing down on her. Instead of darkness now, Em saw Matt lying on the ground, his eyes open, pleading with her to help him. Pink bubbles floated past her eyes. She thought at first that her nose was bleeding, but she looked down at Matt and knew the blood was his.

Oh, Matt!

She was back on her bed, her chin pressed to her chest, drooling on her pajamas.

And the figure was gone.

Em! Em! Are you okay?

Zach charged into Em's room, his blond hair wild, his cricket bat poised above his head.

"My hero," said Em, rolling her eyes. She felt weak. The horned man's presence had taken a lot out of her. "You're too late. He's gone."

Zach looked around in confusion. Em showed him the picture she had drawn. She had caught the man's intense, pleading expression, the colors exploding behind him. He resembled Matt so strongly that it pained her to look at him.

Zach stared at the picture. *A dream?*

It wasn't a dream, Zach. Someone is trying to send me a message.

Zach set the bat next to the bedroom door. *Who?*

Em sat down shakily on the bed. "I don't know," she signed, "yet."

SEVEN

Water began to drop in slices, as if the wave were a loaf of bread on the abbey's kitchen table. Matt realized Jeannie was doing her best to break the wave up, limit its power, before the wall of water collapsed in its fatal entirety.

Draw something.

Digging frantically in his pocket for paper, his eyes stinging from the salt, Matt cursed. His pencil was stuck in the lining and he couldn't grasp it. His fingers were frozen and felt like thumbs. He finally gripped the pencil and began to draw—a rubber raft, the kind that he'd seen helicopters dropping into a stormy ocean to rescue stranded tourists or fishermen in trouble.

As soon as he'd imagined the basic outline of the dinghy, Matt felt himself rising off the sand. In an explosion of yellow and orange light, he dropped snugly into the center of a raft.

It wasn't enough. He kept drawing, shading, sketching, until an inflated dome settled over the raft, sealing itself around the edges with a soft hiss.

Matt was completely cocooned inside his own animation.

He licked the tip of his finger and erased a section of the shaded area on the side of the dome. As he worked, a porthole cut into the real dome and sealed itself with a fizzing zipper of light.

Outside, Matt heard an unearthly roar. The wave was falling.

He drew handles and gripped them tightly. The surging water lifted the dinghy, tossing it far from the beach to land on the hill-side. It bounced, tumbling back on itself, back out over the lip of the shore to slam into the sea.

Matt's stomach was somersaulting. Scrambling toward the little porthole as the water tipped and surged beneath his feet, he pressed his hands to the clear plastic, hunting frantically for Jeannie.

She was still on the hillside, slumped against a pine tree, tied to the trunk by the strings of her safety vest. Jeannie looked to be unconscious and battered, but still breathing.

Matt fell back on the yellow rubber and closed his eyes. Minutes passed as he steadied his breathing. *You're still alive. Jeannie too*. His relief was acute.

He was beginning to feel a bit seasick when rocks and pebbles began slapping the side of the raft with increasing fury. Wiping the condensation from the small porthole with unsteady hands, Matt spotted Carik crouched on the battered shoreline, pulling an arrow from her quiver and taking aim at the raft. Solon was with her, pointing straight at the porthole.

"Aim for its eye, Carik!" Matt heard him shout.

Carik's arrow sliced through the porthole, just missing Matt's shoulder. He shifted as far from the porthole as he could, rummaging in his pocket for his drawing.

"No!" he yelled. "Stop!"

Matt's flailing caused the raft to bounce and roll on the water like a struggling mammal. He had a nasty feeling that his yells sounded like an animal's muffled growls.

"Don't shoot! It's me!"

The drawing must have fallen out when he was being tossed around by the wave. He needed to destroy it, and show Solon and Carik that he was no sea monster. Matt scrambled onto his knees, frantically searching. There it was, caught in the seal between the raft and the dome.

Swoosh. Another arrow flew through the hole, this time tearing his jeans and grazing Matt's thigh.

"OW! Stop!"

Matt lunged flat on the bottom of the raft—and dropped the drawing again.

Outside, Matt could see Solon wading into the water, his eyes fierce and flashing, his sword ready to stab the strange yellow beast through its heart. Matt knew he wouldn't be able to avoid Solon's sword when it pierced the raft. He rolled with all his might until the raft flipped over.

Surprised by the sudden movement, Solon jumped back. Carik ducked behind an outcropping of rocks. As Solon reared back to plunge his sword into the middle of the raft, it burst before his eyes in a blaze of yellow light.

Matt lay gasping on his back on the shoreline, shards of yellow light and clumps of sand raining down on him.

Looking stricken, Solon raced over to help him up. Carik slung her quiver over her shoulder and splashed out into the sea as well. She seized Matt's arm and shook him.

"Did the beast swallow you when the wave fell?" she demanded, looking suspiciously out to sea.

Matt felt an odd mix of pleasure and discomfort from Carik's touch.

"Yes," he replied, laughing for the first time in ages. "I was its lunch."

EIGHT

One of the world's most powerful Guardians, second only to Matt and Em's grandfather Renard, Henrietta de Court was an elegant woman with an extensive knowledge of poisons and a passion for exquisite hats. Today she was wearing a flouncy, feathery one that draped over her high forehead. She also carried a polished wooden cane with a carved peryton at its hilt and an explosive secret.

This morning she was running late for a meeting with Sir Charles in the Council of Guardians' chambers—a confrontation, if she were to be honest, that she'd been putting off for years.

The Council of Guardians had been in existence ever since the formation of the Royal Academy in the 1760s had given English Animare like Sir Joshua Reynolds and Thomas Gainsborough a legitimate means of support for their imaginative capabilities. The Guardians had constructed their original council chambers beneath the Foundling Hospital in Bloomsbury, where the academy had held its first show of work by its members. Up until then, Guardians and Animare in England had been only loosely bound to each other, left to live very much on their own wits, and only formally gathering for two important, timeless rituals: the binding of an Animare whose powers had either grown too strong or were out of control, and the lifelong union of an Animare to his or her Guardian. More than 250 years later, the Guardians had Councils all over the world. The protection of Animare and their valuable talents had remained strong in all that time.

Until now.

Henrietta tutted. Not only was she late, she needed to make a detour to the rare-book library on the third floor before the meeting. Marching toward the entrance to the Royal Academy at Burlington House, she saw the line waiting to clear security and made a quick decision. Dangerous times called for dangerous actions. Rules be damned.

A middle-aged couple looking at a map of the London Underground stood in front of her. Henrietta put her hand on the man's shoulder, sensing in seconds he was hungry and annoyed about waiting in yet another queue. She gently pushed a series of images into his mind—scones topped with jam and clotted cream, steaming cups of tea. His wife blinked a couple of times as Henrietta filled her mind with a fog of confusion.

"The tea shop across the way has such delicious treats," Henrietta murmured.

The man's expression cleared. "I think a cuppa is in order," he said, pulling his wife from the line. Henrietta smiled as they hurried quickly out of the courtyard to the street.

Henrietta worked through the rest of the line more quickly, tickling minds with compassion for the woman in the flouncy hat and an overwhelming desire to let her into the building as quickly as possible. One by one, the line parted and Henrietta glided to the front.

She avoided the busy elevator and marched up the wide stairs to the second floor, the tip of her cane tapping the marble steps like a claw. Ignoring the tourists and one or two artists at work in front of paintings, she carried on through the main hall to a smaller gallery and the entrance to the rare-book room. Taking a quick left at the end of the gallery, Henrietta turned into a narrow anteroom, where she stopped at the security desk.

A girl with short blond hair sat behind the desk. She stood, quickly skimming the names on her list of scholars expected to use the private reading room that day.

"We're not open yet, Professor de Court," she said apologetically, "and I don't believe I have your name on our list."

"Really, Lucy," said Henrietta in her most irritable voice, "is this necessary?"

Turning a little pink, the receptionist picked up her phone. "Let me double-check with Sir Charles," she said.

Henrietta sighed, tapping her cane on the floor. She knew the routine. She'd have to wait for someone from Sir Charles's office to come down and escort her to a table. There, she would be required to fill out a form (in triplicate) and wait for her ID to be checked (twice). And then she'd have to wait for the book she wanted to look at to be delivered to her table, where someone would watch over her as she pulled on the necessary white gloves before turning its delicate pages.

She didn't have time for such bureaucratic nonsense this morning.

For the second time in less than an hour, Henrietta broke the rules. She placed her hand gently on the receptionist's arm and smiled.

Seconds later, the lock on the double glass doors clicked and popped open with a hiss. Henrietta hooked the peryton cane over her forearm and walked sure-footedly into the rare-book room.

NINE

Before the twenty-first century, the rare books housed in the room had been stored behind sliding glass on the original mahogany shelves, and accessed with a key. Although access was limited to authorized scholars and anyone on the Council of Guardians, the parchment on the books and their inks had slowly been losing the battle with time and temperature. Henrietta had insisted that Sir Charles upgrade the environment for the manuscripts, or risk being challenged for leadership of the Council.

She had no intention of removing him from his position until the time was right, but he was not to know that.

Inside the library the rare books and ancient manuscripts were housed in climate-controlled pods behind thick glass on shelves like conveyer belts, allowing the books to be accessed with as little human contact and exposure to the elements as possible.

Henrietta went directly to the control panel and scanned in the receptionist's ID and then her own. When access was granted, she would have about five minutes to find what she was looking for before her ID would be flagged in Sir Charles's office and he'd send someone to find out what she was doing.

Punching in the code she'd memorized, Henrietta stepped back and watched the shelves shift, turn, and orbit the room as if she were watching the inner workings of a great mechanical monster. Once the computer located the book, its shelf shifted forward and the individual case dropped into a tiny transparent elevator.

Henrietta kept one eye on her watch as she watched the shelves turn. After two minutes, the small doors opened before her. Slipping on a pair of white gloves, she lifted the hermetically sealed container to the nearest table.

Inside the container sat a leather-bound, pocket-size book of William Blake's children's poems. Henrietta checked her watch. Two minutes left. Someone would already be on the way. Carefully opening the book, Henrietta slipped her fingers behind the wrinkled spine, grasped a coin between her fingers, and tugged it out of its hiding place.

She'd always thought Malcolm would be at her side when she asserted her leadership at the Council table. Having finally come to terms with his disappearance, she had decided to forge ahead.

She admired the medallion's craftsmanship. There was no reason to leave it hidden any longer.

Outside in the anteroom she could hear the receptionist's voice.

"I'm quite sure no one has entered the room this morning. You must have been alerted in error."

Henrietta slipped the coin under the brim of her hat. Swiftly replacing the book, she closed the container and pushed it back into the chute. She couldn't activate the mechanics of the stacks without the noise giving away her presence, so she left it where it was.

She folded her not-so-lithe body as well as she could under a study carrel just as the library door opened—and just as she spotted her cane, still propped against the table where she'd been working.

"I told you no one has come into the library yet this morning," said the receptionist, glaring at the guard whom Sir Charles had sent to check on the activation of the stacks.

"Just doing my job, miss."

Henrietta inhaled and calmed her mind. It was inevitable that the guard would spot her cane. He was trained for moments like this. She could ill afford the time to explain herself.

Closing her eyes, Henrietta put herself in Lucy's head again.

I'm so sorry, ma chérie.

Lucy fainted, swooning into the arms of the surprised guard.

Somewhere in between more staff rushing in to assist and the medics arriving, Henrietta emerged from beneath the carrel, lifted her cane, and slipped away.

TEN

Carik kicked at a clod of sand freckled with yellow light from the raft. She frowned at Matt. "That was an illumination?"

Matt nodded, scrambling to his feet. "It was the only way to protect myself from the wave. There's no more time to explain." He gazed up at the hillside, at the motionless figure in orange slumped against the tree. "We need to help Jeannie."

A fierce wind gusted along the shore, and for a second the sun disappeared in darkness again. Matt looked up. Carik gasped and stepped closer to Solon.

A shadowy black peryton—its body like obsidian and its wings like crushed velvet—hovered high above Era Mina. Malcolm sat on its broad back, no longer hooded but in polished black leather armor. His shoulder plates were shaped like the peryton's wings, a silver helix shimmering on his breast and his long legs astride the beast's fiery red saddle. An embroidered cover fluttered out behind the saddle like yellow flames. Where the white peryton's antlers were thick and covered in a layer of fur, the black peryton's tines were translucent. A cloaked figure sat bundled up in front of Malcolm.

"It's my dad!" said Matt in horror. "And he has someone else with him!"

"It's too far away for me to tell who it is," said Solon in frustration.

"These will help." Matt handed over Duncan Fox's opera glasses.

Solon studied the opera glasses curiously, then lifted them to his eyes. Almost instantly, he dropped them to the sand with an exclamation.

"It's a special kind of glass," said Matt, grinning.

Even in the tension of the moment, Solon's face was a picture of astonishment. "Not an enchantment?" he said.

"No," said Matt. "Science."

Solon picked up the glasses and looked again. He hissed through his teeth and lowered them.

"Your father's captive is the abbot," he said, and shoved the glasses into Matt's hands.

"I'm really sorry," Matt said, grimacing with guilt. "This is all my fault."

Carik fitted an arrow into her bow and pointed it at Matt's chest. "This boy has brought this evil here," she said. "We should kill him now."

Matt's heart thumped like a drum in his chest. Carik was right. If he hadn't been in such a frenzy to bring Malcolm back in time to rescue Em and his mum, his dad would never have been able to seize the opportunity to implement a plan that had been festering in his mind for years.

Matt tried inspiriting her, breaking up her anger before she let her arrow fly. "You don't want to hurt me, Carik—"

"Do not try your enchantments on me," she interrupted with a hiss, drawing back her bow arm. Matt held his breath.

Solon rested his hand on Carik's arm, keeping it there until she reluctantly lowered her bow. Matt breathed again.

Malcolm and the peryton still hovered high above them.

"The abbot is my master's Guardian, Brother Renard," said Solon. "Brother Renard's mind is fragile. He needs the abbot to keep him calm, to prevent him from animating unwittingly. If your father has the abbot, what has become of my master?"

Picking up the opera glasses, Matt looked at his dad circling in and out of the scudding clouds above the bay. His mouth went dry.

Malcolm Calder was a disturbing sight. His head was bare, but even his long dark curls couldn't hide his grotesque face. His eyes were blazing with a passion Matt found almost as frightening as the red unfinished flesh of his cheek and the exposed white bone of his jaw.

"The black peryton looks—ghostly," said Matt, swallowing. "Like my father's riding a specter."

Solon yanked his sword from the hard sand. "The legend states that the white peryton abandoned his brother in the icy north, and all that remains on these islands is the black beast's shadow. Both beasts can only be called forth by a descendant of Albion, the First Animare. The man who started *The Book of Beasts*. The man who founded the monastery."

Matt remembered how he and Em had called the white peryton to help *them*. If the perytons only responded to descendants of this Albion, he and Em must be descendants of Albion too. And Jeannie? She had controlled the wave. Was she connected to the islands and the perytons in the same way?

Matt's heart twisted as he looked up the hillside toward Jeannie, curled in an awkward position by the tree, her legs bent underneath her.

She'll be okay, he told himself fiercely.

He needed to do something, to confront his father and free the abbot. He needed a weapon of some kind—but what? What could he draw on? He shoved his hands into his damp pockets. He didn't have any paper left.

His dad and the black peryton dropped closer, gusting cold air across the beach.

"Find a weapon, Matt!" shouted Solon, raising his sword.

Matt felt a surge of brutality in the air, cruelty so dreadful it slammed into him, knocking him to his knees. He was no longer thinking about drawing.

"My father is about to do something terrible," he said as evenly as he could. He started running up the beach. "I can feel it. We need to get Jeannie away from here."

"*No!*" cried Solon in anguish.

Matt stumbled in surprise, turned back, looked up.

The abbot was tumbling like Icarus toward the sea.

ELEVEN

The Royal Academy

London

Present Day

When Henrietta de Court entered the suite of private rooms belonging to the Council of Guardians on the second floor of the Royal Academy, the room was empty, Sir Charles having gone to see for himself that all was well in the rare-book room. She was alone.

Seating herself at the head of the long mahogany table that filled the room, Henrietta unpinned her hat and set it on the chair next to her. Her fingers played with her pearl hat pin for a few seconds, then stabbed it through the elegant chignon on the nape of her neck lest she lose it.

The Council chambers' high walls were its most striking feature, adorned as they were with images of the most fantastic beasts ever imagined. A snakelike basilisk whose gaze was fatal.

A kraken whose monstrous tentacles could sink a hundred ships. Sirens with inspiriting abilities as powerful as hers. Then there were selkies and sea serpents, wraiths and hydras, gorgons and griffins. All the creatures immortalized here had been trapped in Hollow Earth since the monks of Auchinmurn had drawn them into a sacred illuminated manuscript, locking them away from the uncomprehending eyes of a Christian world. One day they would be free again. That day was coming with or without her son's help; Henrietta could feel it.

She gazed thoughtfully across the table at the medieval tapestry covering the far wall. Known as *The Battle for Era Mina*, the tapestry showed the grendel, an apelike monster, rising out of a dark swamp to devour the dead after a terrible battle. The central figure, a hooded monk draped in dark velvet, was riding a black stallion, exhorting ghastly troops of skeletons to do his bidding. It was awe inspiring in its detail, its ferocity, and its glowing jewel-like colors. Even more remarkable was the fact that it had been woven more than seven hundred years earlier, by the monks of Auchinmurn.

There was still no sign of Sir Charles. To pass the time, Henrietta left the table to study the tapestry in more detail.

The wool and silk threads crisscrossed in vibrant reds, blues, and golds as they told their gory story. Tapestries such as this one were like news reports for an event, a means for a community to record history before cameras or cell phones or even paper. With the tip of her finger, Henrietta traced a single silk thread along the edge of the great stitched cloth, stopping to admire the complex pattern that had captured the drama of the battle.

Hearing voices in the outer office, Henrietta made to return to the table. As she lifted her fingers from the tapestry, the threads she had been tracing began to glow, faintly at first but then more brightly. Instinctively, Henrietta looked at her hand. It was clean and appeared normal. Was this her doing?

Another thread lit up, and another, and another. Soon the entire tapestry was illuminated as if it had been plugged in, an electrified subway map with every thread a pulsing track.

Henrietta ran to the double doors and locked them before Sir Charles could come in. She stood back and watched the tapestry in awe.

The illuminated threads, first one at a time and then in patterns of three, four, and five from every section of the narrative, unraveled, changing routes, taking new directions, and twisting into new patterns as the entire tapestry was rewoven in front of Henrietta's eyes. In their new positions, all the threads blazed, and then in the same instant were dim again. The history that the tapestry was depicting had changed.

Henrietta stood absolutely still, absorbing every detail of the newly woven version of events. When her eyes rested on the imposing figure at the center of the picture, she laughed aloud and clapped her hands in rapturous applause.

She had just witnessed one of the most spectacular feats of animation ever accomplished. It would change everything. *Every-*

thing. She didn't need Sir Charles or the Council of Guardians anymore. It was time to move from the shadows into the light.

To give her only son the power he deserved.

"I knew you hadn't abandoned me, Malcolm my love, my dear boy." Her voice was spiked with adoration, adrenaline, and years of repressed ambition. "You have achieved the unimaginable. Done the impossible. Now let me help you."

She could not leave the tapestry here. She could not let anyone else see how it had changed until she was ready.

Dragging a chair over, she climbed up and unhooked the cloth from its iron rod. It was heavy, and required all her strength. Hastily, she rolled it like a carpet, using the belt from her coat to keep it secure. She ran to the windows on the other side of the room and threw them open. Dragging and pulling the tapestry toward the biggest window, she heaved it over the sill into a private courtyard a short distance below. It fell to the ground with a weighty thud.

The door handles rattled.

"Henrietta!" called Sir Charles through the wood. "Why is this door locked? Are you ill? Open these doors immediately."

A euphoric Henrietta pinned on her hat, grabbed her cane, and climbed out the window after her prize.

TWELVE

Malcolm's cruel intentions were suffocating Matt, slowing him down. Beneath the bile, the cold, unyielding rage, Matt had sensed his father's true focus.

Malcolm tugged on the black peryton's antlers. The beast reared, racing through the clouds toward the blackened hillside and the feebly stirring form of the abbey's housekeeper.

"He's coming for you!" yelled Solon behind Matt. "Take cover!"

"He wants Jeannie!" yelled Matt. He had left the soft sand now and was scrambling to pull himself up and over the lip of the hill. "He needs her. I can feel it. Jeannie!" he screamed, clawing his way up the impossible slope. "Wake up! You have to move!"

Malcolm and the black peryton were flying fast and low across the surf now, the beast's hooves sparking against the outcropping rocks and the tips of its wings whipping the tips of the waves. Matt lunged at a tree root to heave himself farther up the treacherous slope, but it popped like a loose tooth in his hands, dropping him desperately, maddeningly onto the sand again.

Carik shot three arrows in quick succession at Malcolm and the demonic specter. The wind and her terror distorted her aim, and the arrows veered harmlessly into the water. The beast was almost upon them, its spectral form gleaming, its wide, snorting nostrils and its blazing eyes terrifying to behold.

Matt got to his feet, shaking and battered, searching hopelessly for some means of scaling the smooth, unforgiving, muddy slope that lay between him and Jeannie.

"I'll hoist you up!" Solon shouted, cupping his hands.

With Solon's assistance, Matt made it over the lip of the muddy hillside. He scrambled to get a hold, shoving his hands deeper and deeper into the swampy ground, cold mud up to his elbows as he clawed his way forward. He couldn't slip again.

Up ahead, Jeannie was fumbling to free herself from the tree. She wasn't making progress. Her hands were swollen and red and the knots in her apron had tightened with the water.

"Son," she said groggily, seeing Matt pounding and slipping toward her. "This isn't yer fight. Find yer way home."

A dark shadow swept over them.

"Dad!" Matt was struggling to stand in the streaming mud. "Don't hurt her! Don't hurt Jeannie!"

Malcolm and the beast hovered above Jeannie and Matt, the

wind from the peryton's wings forcing Jeannie back against the tree. Malcolm grinned, the stretch of his lips tearing into the powdery pink flesh, exposing the black roots of his missing teeth and dripping clots of ink from his chin onto the winged collar of his chain mail.

"Don't hurt her, Dad," Matt screamed.

Jeannie blinked up at Malcolm. "You hurt the wean, Malcolm Calder," she hissed, "and it'll be your death too."

Down below, Carik and Solon had waded out into the water for the motionless body of the abbot as he drifted in to the shore. Now they were lifting him from the waves.

"I'll do anything you want, Dad!" Matt yelled, shoving his arms and legs deep into the mud to anchor himself.

Mesmerized, he watched his father tug the peryton higher, swinging some kind of lasso in tight circles above his head. A black orb the size of a football attached to the end of the rope flew toward Jeannie's head, where it whirred and clicked and popped open, dropping a mechanical net over her. The sides snapped against each other like teeth, locking Jeannie inside.

How is he doing this? Matt wondered, lunging toward the swinging net.

He wasn't fast enough. Malcolm and the beast galloped away through the air, dragging Jeannie behind them, vanishing into the clouds and leaving a ragged line of light like a scar in the sky.

THIRTEEN

Matt's body was caked in filth, his hair stuck to his scalp in thick clumps. A cut on his cheek was bleeding. But it was the pain inside his head that was making his teeth ache. He had failed.

He walked in defeat across the beach to where Solon was kneeling next to the abbot. Matt had never seen a dead body before. He slowed, unsure of what to expect.

Solon had pulled the abbot's hood respectfully over his face, leaving only the old man's pale chin and wiry gray whiskers visible beneath the folds of cloth. His hands were tucked inside his sleeves and his arms folded in front of him, his wet robes clinging to the body like a heavy skin. It was clear that the fall into the sea from such a great height had broken him.

"We must get his body somewhere dry and safe." Solon's voice was thick. "After we find Brother Renard, we will lay the abbot to rest. Then we deal with your father."

Matt kneeled next to Solon, feeling more desperate than ever. "That man, that monster is not my father. Whatever happened when I . . . I brought him here destroyed his mind . . . or whatever was left of it."

"No matter. He will pay." Solon stood. "Help me carry the abbot to higher ground. We must lay him somewhere safe, where hungry animals can't touch him."

Matt silently reached for a stick and sketched in the dry, hard-packed sand above the tide line. Within seconds a simple plank coffin appeared.

"You have broken the rules again," said Solon after a moment.

"This is no time for rules," said Matt.

Together they lifted the abbot inside the coffin. Solon dug around in the rocks until he found two flat stones, and placed them gently and reverently on the abbot's eyes. Matt dropped the heavy lid.

"It should keep out any animals until we can bury him properly," said Matt.

Carik suddenly came sprinting around the rocky point.

"RUN!" she screamed.

A line of knights in matching black armor, wings forged on their shoulders and silver spirals on their breastplates, was marching swiftly toward them. Their heads were cowled in chain mail, and each figure was outlined in an eerie yellow light.

"Animations!" said Matt in astonishment, scrambling to his feet. His father couldn't have imagined this army. He was only a Guardian. Who had created them?

They were six knights, each one at least two meters tall and moving fast, marching with unnatural speed and an extraordinary choreographed precision, their bony joints visible through the chain mail. But it was their heads that horrified Matt.

Each had only half a face.

Matt's first idea was to imagine a machine gun, but he knew he couldn't. Gunpowder wouldn't make its way to the far corners of Scotland for another century at least, never mind rapid-fire guns. He'd already violated history enough. What could he do to fight these creatures?

Carik leaped up onto a ridge of rocks and released a flurry of arrows, hitting one or two of the knights in the back and puncturing their armor. The resulting wounds oozed a thick, bubbling black liquid onto the sand, melting everything it touched as the knight dissolved to a hissing puddle.

"Don't let that stuff touch you!" Matt yelled at Carik in warning.

It was too late. Carik screamed in pain when one of the creatures turned toward her, splashing the oozing tar on her hand and blistering the skin on contact.

"It's some kind of incendiary ink, like sulfur and coal tar," Matt began to explain. "It probably burned her, but Carik's going to be—"

With a feral howl Solon had already charged among the six remaining skeletal soldiers, swinging and thrusting his broadsword, reducing one to fizzling liquid with a lucky stab to the image on its breastplate.

"Aim for the breastplate!" he shouted, wiping the ink on his clothing.

Instantly the liquid ate through the wool of Solon's tunic. Matt could smell burning flesh as Solon screamed. Frantically the young monk ripped the burning cloth from his body and grabbed a handful of wet seaweed, pressing it hard against the smoldering wound.

The remaining knights now homed in on Matt, who had scrambled onto the jagged rocks that lined the shore. With no time to think any longer, Matt used the tip of Solon's knife to scratch a weapon on the face of the rock.

This had better work.

FOURTEEN

A motorized hum electrified the air seconds before a double-ended lightsaber materialized in Matt's hand. He stumbled a little at first, not realizing how heavy his creation would be, but quickly adjusted, checked his stance, and tightened his grip on the central handle. Dropping one shoulder, he swooped at the faceless knight on his left, plunging the end of the laser into his breastplate, then pivoted and plunged the other side into a second creature approaching from the right. Each dissolved into pools of thick black ink at the base of the rocks.

Two more flew at him. Matt sidestepped the first, slipped on a slick rock, but righted himself in time to plunge his laser into its chest before he went down. The other end of the lightsaber missed the second completely, and Matt landed in a spreading puddle of burning ink.

"Ow!"

The toxic mixture singed through Matt's jeans. He rolled away, his whole body shrieking with pain. The last knight's rotting face was almost upon him. Matt got to his knees, twisted around, and swung his laser at its head. He missed.

It was Solon who leaped up onto the rocks to stab his sword into the last faceless knight's back and out through his chest.

The two boys leaned against each other next to the abbot's coffin, catching their breath, watching the ink simmer and seep into the sand.

Solon stared at Matt's lightsaber in awe. "Is this a weapon from your time?"

"It's from a galaxy far, far away," said Matt, grinning.

"Where did you learn to fight like that?" asked Carik, letting Solon plaster seaweed onto her blistering hand. It was clear that she was trying not to appear impressed.

Matt pressed the button in the center, and the lightsabers withdrew into their respective sides of the handle. "Video games," he said, scraping his drawing off the rock. With a soft hum, the weapon vanished, leaving a faint green glow floating above his hands that faded into nothing. "You play with an avatar on a . . . a special screen against the avatars of other gamers. This weapon is from a game with Jedi knights."

Matt caught Carik and Solon exchanging glances, and sensed

that they were communicating telepathically, most likely dis-cussing how they apparently still had knights in the future. It reminded Matt of how alone he was. He missed having Em in his head, even when she wasn't speaking to him. Her presence had been comforting. Matt trusted he'd feel something much worse than this emptiness if Em really was dead.

Surely he would know. He would feel *something*.

One thing Matt did know for sure. His mum and Em weren't in the Middle Ages anymore.

"What is an avatar?" asked Solon.

Matt forced his mind back to the present. "It's a thing that you create . . . to fight for you in games."

Solon's face cleared. "Like a squire taking a knight's place at a joust?"

"Sort of," said Matt, deciding that explaining online gaming and the Internet to two medieval teenagers centuries before the printing press and movable type would take too much energy.

The tide had come in, leaving only a narrow strip of jag-ged rocks, like uneven teeth, exposed beneath the hillside. The abbot's coffin lay perilously close to the edge of the water.

"We can't leave the coffin here," said Solon, assessing the water. "The abbot would be washed out to sea with the tide."

"Wouldn't that be honorable?" asked Carik. "All my people are returned to the sea in flames. It's how they journey to Val-halla."

Solon shook his head. "The abbot has a place in the crypt with the other great monks of Era Mina. He has earned that honor. We must put him somewhere safe before we seek shelter ourselves."

Struggling against the rising wind and the dropping temperatures, the boys got a grip on each end of the coffin without either one of them falling into the bay. Stepping with great care from rock to rock, they followed Carik to the end of the cove where there was a rocky ledge high and wide enough for them to hoist the abbot's coffin to safety.

Free of their burden, the three of them picked up their pace, hugging the rock face for cover as they hurried along the narrow exposed strip of beach, heading to the other side of the island to take shelter in the old smugglers' caves.

FIFTEEN

H unt her down, Vaughn," Sir Charles had instructed through tight lips, his hand already on the phone to convene an emergency meeting of the European Council of Guardians. "Whatever it takes, find Henrietta de Court and that tapestry."

Hunting rogue Guardians and Animare was familiar ground to Vaughn Grant. As an agent of Orion, the secret organization of Animare hunters scattered throughout the world, Vaughn spent much of his time on similar missions. It was how he had reconnected with Sandie, after Sir Charles had charged him with tracking her and the twins when she had gone into hiding in the early days.

He'd done his job too well back then. Rather than betray Sandie, he had helped her survive. It was at that time Vaughn had also agreed to help Renard, his friend and mentor, by spying on Sir Charles and watching over Sandie and the twins.

This mission, however, felt more serious than most. Henrietta de Court was one of the most senior Guardians on the European Council. The remaining members of the European Council would need at least a day to answer Sir Charles's summons and gather at the Royal Academy, but Vaughn didn't need to wait.

Glancing at his watch for the tenth time in as many minutes, Vaughn wondered if he would make it to the National Gallery of Scotland before it closed for the night. It was already 4:40 p.m., and he was still in London. He had twenty minutes left in which to do it.

It was dangerous, but not impossible.

He stared irritably at the group of schoolgirls who'd broken away from the last public tour of the day to root themselves in front of the painting Vaughn needed. Samuel Morse's *Gallery of the Louvre* was a large painting that stretched across most of the wall between the Royal Academy's two primary staircases. Vaughn tried to will the girls away from the art, but he was not a Guardian. Inspiriting them to move from the painting wasn't in his skill set.

Adrenaline surged through Vaughn's veins. He let it. He'd need every bit of energy for what he was about to do.

"This is the one I wanted to tell you about," said a curly haired redhead to her classmates in a loud voice.

A dark-haired girl jabbed in the direction of the painting with her pen. "Looks lame to me," she said.

The redhead folded her arms. "You're just annoyed because Mr. James put me in charge of our group for a change."

Vaughn leaned forward, glancing down the hallway. *Come on, girls, please move.* Opening and closing his fists, he cracked his knuckles in the ready. His stomach rumbled, and a headache was starting to pound behind his temples. He couldn't remember the last time he'd eaten. Tapas near the Prado in Madrid yesterday? Or was that the day before?

"The artist painted a room at the Louvre and put all his favorite pictures on its walls," the redhead continued as the pen-wielding girl grumbled on. "See there's the *Mona Lisa* next to the door and the—"

"That's really not where the *Mona Lisa* is in the Louvre," snapped the pen girl. "I've seen it."

"That's not the point," said the redhead stubbornly. "The point is . . . this painting is *haunted*. My sister's friend knows one of the night guards. He's seen things."

"Will all patrons begin to make their way to the exits," boomed the public address system as the girls exploded with laughter. "The Royal Academy of Arts will be closing promptly in fifteen minutes."

Vaughn knew he was cutting this far too close. He'd made the journey from London to Edinburgh in nine minutes once, but his mind had been sharper then, and his imagination singularly focused. Unlike this afternoon. He'd already been traveling for close to thirty-six hours, and a lack of sleep compounded with his worry—about the twins, about Sandie, about Henrietta de Court—

meant he was exhausted. An exhausted Animare could screw up, and a screwup when traveling by these means could be dangerous. Even fatal.

"My sister's friend," continued the redhead, raising her voice over the disbelieving laughter, "said that sometimes the guard can hear laughing and giggling from the painting and—"

"What utter rubbish," the pen-holding girl said scornfully, flouncing toward the stairs with the others.

If Vaughn arrived after the National Gallery in Edinburgh closed, he'd have to animate something to avoid triggering the alarms or arousing their guards, and the more he had to animate when he was feeling this drained, the riskier it was. Vaughn glanced at his watch again.

The redhead shoved her gallery map into her backpack and stomped after the others. "Yeah, well . . . the artist who painted this invented Morse code. And that's amazing," she shouted after them, grasping for one last tidbit before she lost her audience entirely. "And if it wasn't for him, well . . . well, we wouldn't have . . . have . . . smart phones."

At last they were gone. Vaughn stood, stretched, slipped on his leather jacket, and pulled his messenger bag over his shoulder. Checking that the hallway was completely empty, he stepped in front of Morse's painting.

The *Gallery of the Louvre* had never brought Samuel Morse the fame he'd hoped as an artist, but it had brought him a more important kind of renown. Morse had used his unique abilities as an Animare and a code maker to serve a greater cause. Thanks to Morse's skills, Vaughn and a small number of uniquely trained Animare were able to travel between various Guardian Councils and galleries. Because of Morse, a series of paintings around the world were linked to this painting as a kind of hub.

Vaughn slipped his sketchbook from his messenger bag and began to draw. Those girls would never know it, but the redhead was on to something about the nature of the painting. Haunted wasn't even the half of it.

SIXTEEN

First Vaughn sketched *The Wedding Feast at Cana*, the canvas that covered the entire wall on the left side of Morse's painting. Then the Titians, the Van Dycks, Raphael, and Rubens—all with the kind of detail that anyone watching would have thought only possible after long hours, perhaps even days, of work. For Vaughn, his copy of the painting took shape quickly, his fingers flying across the page.

Only trained Orion agents were able to travel across art in this way. At least that's how it used to be. Sandie and the twins had done the impossible, circumventing Orion agents' training and traveling through art by their own means. If the Hollow Earth Society or even the world's five Councils of Guardians discovered that the twins and Sandie could fade across not only paintings but time as well, life as they knew it would be over.

Vaughn could not let that happen.

The light around Vaughn began to soften, bathing him in a buttery haze, its illumination suffusing every part of his body, slowly muting his physical presence while he sketched on. Sounds muffled in Vaughn's mind as if all his senses were fluid. He relaxed and let his imagination assume control.

It was at that moment it all went wrong.

A horrified scream cut through the thinning sounds of the gallery, snapping Vaughn's concentration. He hesitated, his fingers lifting off the page for only a beat, but long enough. His imagination stalled, his pulse plummeted. Every particle of his being exploded in pain. He collapsed to his knees on the floor, in agony as every nerve ending sparked and snapped and shot bolts of light through his body.

He was burning up from the inside.

He caught a glimpse of his reflection in the windows. His body looked like the negative of a photograph, a profile of light and dark against a halo of fading light, and his eyes were a fiery red. Crumpled on the floor, his body spasming against the pain, Vaughn glanced toward the stairs and saw the pen-holding girl staring in terror at his electrified silhouette.

"I dropped my p . . . p . . . pen . . ." she stuttered, her eyes wide and disbelieving. With a final piercing scream, she dropped her schoolbag and took off down the stairs.

Her panic would bring security guards and questions. Lots of questions. Too much was at stake for that to happen. Vaughn had to get into Morse's painting, or he had to destroy himself before the guards reached him. It was what was expected of an agent when caught.

Vaughn focused first on his hands, willing them to move, to draw again. If he couldn't regain control, his entire being would implode.

Ignoring the heat searing into his bones, he struggled to his knees and then to his feet, with a burst of strength that fueled rather than drained him.

Draw!

Forcing everything but Morse's painting from his imagination, slowly, carefully, painfully, Vaughn willed his blistered fingers to move again, to shade the arched doorway of the Louvre at the center of the painting, to outline the Roman statue of Diana, the goddess of the hunt, in the corner, to scribble the men and women in the forefront. And with every curving line, every shade, streak, and stipple from his charcoal, Vaughn felt the heat dissipate, felt his heart rate rise and his bones cool. When he glanced at his hands, his skin was translucent, the smoky fog of light finally starting to absorb him.

He hadn't faded completely yet, and he could hear a mob of questioning voices approaching. Time was running out. Vaughn inhaled a deep, soul-filling breath and closed his eyes, sketching the rest of the painting from memory, hoping it would be enough.

In front of him the *Gallery of the Louvre* began to pulse, as if inhaling and exhaling color and light. Slowly at first, then faster, until the images in the painting were bursting from the canvas, cascading over Vaughn, reaching across space and touching, melding with the corresponding images on his sketch.

The mob was almost at the top of the stairs. He was at the point of no return.

Ribbons of reds and yellows, greens and blacks raked over Vaughn. At that precise moment and not a second before, he began to fade, lifting off the ground in a cyclone of color.

In a snap of a second, Vaughn materialized next to James Fenimore Cooper, one of the figures in the corner of the painting, leaving two security guards, a curator, and a schoolteacher puzzling over a set of smoking black burn marks in the gallery floor.

SEVENTEEN

A h, sir, you have returned."

James Fenimore Cooper bowed to Vaughn, handing him a clean handkerchief from the pocket of his topcoat. The other figures in the painting took no notice of the visitor to their gallery, intent instead on their own conversations, except for the artist himself, Samuel Morse, leaning over his wife's shoulder in the painting's foreground. He nodded and smiled at Vaughn.

"I can't stay," replied Vaughn, wiping charcoal and paint dust from his face with Cooper's kerchief.

Cooper bowed again and returned to instructing his wife on the details of the canvas before her, while his daughter kept her admiring eyes on the handsome stranger darting across the gallery.

Even knowing that time had stopped, Vaughn still looked at his watch. Time was a temporal element, and art transcended time. When an Animare faded, he arrived the moment he left. This meant two minutes remained to get to the gallery in Edinburgh before it closed for the day.

Behind the Roman statue of Diana's marble plinth, Vaughn found the canvas he needed tucked out of sight. Despite his throbbing fingers and his bleary eyes, he began to draw himself into another work of art, one that hung in a small rotunda at the National Gallery of Scotland.

When Vaughn burst onto the ice at Duddingston Loch, he first appeared in grays and whites, then quickly added bursts of color and lines of movement. In those first few seconds, he admired the wintery scene emerging before him, the frozen lake nestled in the highlands and the lone skater, a minister, hands clasped behind his back, skating in silence.

Vaughn skidded across the frozen surface of Henry Raeburn's iconic Scottish painting, arms and legs akimbo, struggling to maintain his balance while at the same time punching himself into two, then three, dimensions.

The ice was slicker than Vaughn remembered, and the thick soles on his Doc Martens couldn't stop his momentum. Sliding wildly past the skating minister, Vaughn caught the reverend's eye for a brief moment, then bounced and tumbled across the frozen loch, desperately tearing up his sketch of the work before he crashed into the trees bordering the lake.

In the painting's foreground the reverend cut a comfortable circle on the ice, ignoring Vaughn as he shot out of the landscape and crashed clumsily onto the Edinburgh gallery floor.

EIGHTEEN

While Vaughn was skidding across the frozen loch, Em and Zach were in the abbey library. Since losing Matt, they had spent a lot of time in here, trying to find some means of returning to the past hidden in the musty pages and tooled leather covers of the books that Matt had been studying before he disappeared. They weren't having much luck.

Em had been sidetracked that afternoon, trying to discover something about the mysterious vision in her bedroom. She was convinced he had been trying to tell her about Matt or Jeannie. They were in dreadful danger; she knew it.

I have to do this my own way, she thought. A plan had started to take shape in her mind, but it would require secrecy. Even from Zach. She had no more time to think or plan. Tonight she would act. And if it worked, she'd have Matt and Jeannie home by the weekend.

Zach jabbed her in the arm, making her look up.

"Have you found anything?" he signed.

She laid her book to one side and waved at the artifacts, sketches, and maps strewn across the table. "These are all nineteenth-century copies of medieval maps and texts. At best they'll take us back to Victorian times." She gave a growl of frustration. "I would do *anything* to bring Matt and Jeannie home."

Zach raised his eyebrows. "What about your dad?"

Em snorted. "I hope his hellhounds have him for lunch."

"You don't mean that," signed Zach, leaning back on his chair.

Em flipped open her sketchpad, to a drawing of the abbey as she remembered it from the Middle Ages. If her plan was to work, and there were no guarantees, this drawing had to be as precise and detailed as possible. "Dad tried to use Matt and me to get into Hollow Earth when we were toddlers," she reminded Zach. "He took over our minds and made us draw for him. He could have injured us, but did he care? How is that even close to normal parenting behavior? And now he's doing the same in the Middle Ages. All for the sake of a bunch of monsters buried in the earth! It's insane. *He's* insane."

Em used the edge of her pencil and began to shade the abbey's tower in her drawing. She thought she had got that right.

I'm going to save them by myself.

Zach sat up instantly. *No you're not. You promised.*

Em cursed herself for not concealing her thoughts more carefully. When Zach was concentrating on her like now, it was almost impossible to hide things from him. She focused on emptying her mind before he sensed what she was really up to.

Em . . .

She looked innocently at him. "What?"

Before Zach could reply, they both heard a motorcycle roaring to a stop in the front courtyard.

"Vaughn's back," said Em, pushing away from the table and rushing out of the library's double doors. She paused, looking back at Zach. "You coming?"

In the wood-paneled foyer of the abbey, Vaughn had dropped his helmet and leather jacket on the floor and was greeting Em's mum, Sandie, with a kiss. Em flew at them from the library doors.

"You're still here, Em?" Vaughn laughed, sweeping her off her feet. "I thought you'd be back in the thirteenth century by now."

Sandie slapped Vaughn's shoulder. "Not funny. Do not put that thought in her head."

Em reminded herself that Vaughn was an Animare without Guardian mind-reading abilities. "I promised I wouldn't break any rules for at least a few more days."

"Good girl."

As Vaughn pulled Zach into an embrace, Em saw him mouth something that looked like "Keeping her close?" Seeing it hardened her resolve.

"I've news," Vaughn said, hustling all of them into the kitchen. "Where's Renard? And your dad, Zach?"

"Good news?" said Sandie, smiling in weak hope.

Vaughn squeezed her hand and shook his head. "I wish it was," he said grimly. "But Renard and Simon aren't going to like it one bit."

Em's stomach plummeted. Her brother was already lost in the Middle Ages, facing a monster in the form of his own father. And Vaughn had more bad news?

She couldn't bear to think what it might be.

NINETEEN

When Zach's dad, Simon, and Renard joined them in the kitchen, Em was already seated at the table with a glass of juice, tapping her foot furiously to distract herself from imagining all the terrible things Vaughn might have discovered.

Both men looked tense. The skin under Em's grandfather's eyes was gray and his hair was sticking up in white tufts. His and Simon's anxiety hit Em in a mash-up of emotions, and she tapped her foot even faster.

Sitting beside her, Renard placed a calming hand on Em's knee. Em stopped bouncing her foot and exhaled slowly.

"Tell us what you've discovered," said Renard, looking directly at Vaughn.

Vaughn rolled up his shirtsleeves, accepting a cup of tea from Simon.

"This morning Henrietta de Court stole the *Battle for Era Mina* tapestry from the Council chambers."

The reaction was electric.

Simon put his head in his hands. Sandie choked on her tea. Renard slammed his hand on the table, spilling Em's juice, then leaped to his feet and began pacing the room. Simon grabbed a handful of napkins from the counter, handing them to Zach to mop up the mess, and pounded Sandie on the back to ease her choking.

"I knew that woman could not stay out of our lives," snarled Renard.

Em had never seen such rage on her grandfather's face.

"Who is Henrietta de Court?" she asked tentatively.

It didn't take sophisticated Guardian powers to detect the look that shot among the adults in the room.

"Henrietta de Court is a powerful Guardian," said Sandie in a hoarse voice, wiping tears from her cheeks. "She is also . . . your grandmother."

Em felt as if she had been punched in the stomach. "Are you *kidding* me?"

What is wrong *with this family?* she thought in fury. *When will they stop keeping secrets from me?*

She pushed her chair back, toppling it with a loud crash, and stomped outside to the patio, afraid of what she might say and animate with so much adrenaline and anger surging through her system. She squeezed her hands into fists, digging her nails into her skin.

The evening sky looked as bruised as Em felt. The sun was setting behind the small island with lines of orange, yellow, and purple streaking across the horizon.

She wanted to punch something. She wanted to scream. So she did. She gave a shriek so loud and piercing that it rattled the glass doors behind her. A shriek for her own powerlessness, for her grief for Matt and Jeannie.

When she finally quieted, her face was red and her throat was raw. She felt better, calmer and in control. Taking a long, deep breath, she unclenched her fists and loosened her neck muscles. Then she turned and marched back inside.

She glared first at her mother, and then at Renard. "When exactly were you planning to tell me that we . . . that I have a living grandmother?"

"It's not an easy conversation to have," said Sandie. "Your father's mother is not a friend of ours."

Did you know about this, Zach?

Em was shocked to see how pale and trembling Zach was. She realized with a stab of guilt that her explosive tantrum had sliced through his mind like a cleaver. His response to her inquiry was faint.

News to me, too.

Em was filled with remorse. *I'm so sorry. Are you okay?*

I will be. But don't do that again without a warning.

Em sat down, and looked searchingly at the adults. "Explain," she said.

"Don't look at me," Simon said, catching Sandie's glance. "I never wanted to keep Henrietta a secret in the first place."

"Henrietta and I never got along," said Renard finally. "And she wanted to travel, to see the world. . . . She did not want to live here for longer than she had to. One day she packed up and left with your dad when he was about five or six. I remained here."

"Why didn't you go with them?"

This time the emotions among the adults were subtler, complex and confusing. Em needed to use her Guardian abilities to catch the full range and depth of them. A volatile mix of regret and revenge was the strongest, but there were other emotions too difficult to describe. They were emanating most strongly from Renard and Vaughn. The best Em could come up with was a discordant mash-up of loathing and longing.

Do you feel that?

Zach gave a subtle nod. *It's like love and hate at the same time. Is that possible?*

"Please, Renard . . . Grandpa," said Em, holding her grandfather's attention in her mind, gently soothing it. "Tell me everything."

Renard gave a throaty guffaw that flushed his gray face with color and animated his worried eyes. "Emily Calder, are you trying to inspirit me?"

Em flushed as Vaughn started to laugh. Then Simon and Sandie. Soon everyone was roaring, and the tension of the past half hour was broken.

"Not cool, Em." Vaughn grinned. "But awesome for trying."

TWENTY

When the laughter settled, Renard clasped his hands on the table. "I did not leave the island and travel with your grandmother for two significant reasons," he said. "First, I thought that your father would be better living with his mother for a while, and seeing the world while he could."

An odd use of words, Em thought.

"Malcolm was schooled in Paris, Berlin, and Hong Kong," Renard continued. "He lived in Brazil and Bangkok and he grew up to be an excellent Guardian." He hesitated. "Or so I thought."

Vaughn jumped in. "We have recently had confirmation that Henrietta had been planning a coup among Guardians for decades, and grooming Malcolm to lead it. I believe that when Malcolm discovered that Hollow Earth was not just a story, he shared the information with Henrietta. For her, the power and wealth that controlling such an enchanted place would give them . . . I think it was irresistible."

"What was the second significant reason?" signed Zach.

"I cannot travel," Renard said after a moment. "At least, not for as long as Henrietta would have had me do."

"But you're always traveling!" Em said in surprise.

As she spoke she realized Renard hadn't left the island since Jeannie and Matt's disappearance.

"The treasures created by Animare that we keep in the abbey vault cannot be left unattended," said Renard. "A direct descendant of the island's First Animare, Albion, must be present on Auchinmurn at all times to fulfill this duty. In past years, Jeannie and I have shared that responsibility. In fairness, I couldn't leave her alone for that length of time. Now, with Jeannie gone, I bear the responsibility alone. The islands' connection to our kind, and our connection to the islands, are supernatural, intensely powerful, and never to be neglected."

Em tried making sense of this information. "You and Jeannie are both descendants of Albion?"

"We are. It has never seemed like a burden, until recently. But as long as Jeannie is gone, then I must be here."

"Dumb rule," Em scoffed. "Who decided that was the way it had to be? What would happen if you left?"

"I would die," Renard said simply. "The islands would die too, along with whatever else they are protecting."

The import of Renard's words hit Em hard.

Sandie took Em's hand. "You and Matt are descendants of Albion too, Emmie."

Em's eyes widened. Her mum hadn't called her that in ages.

"Does that mean Matt and I can never leave the islands? That we're trapped here for our whole lives?"

"Not as long as Jeannie and I are alive," said Renard.

Em needed to move around, to think this through. She got up from the table and walked over to the model of the abbey in the Middle Ages, which sat on a table in the corner of the kitchen. Matt and Zach had been working on it since they'd come to the island, and it was perfect in every detail. Renard had always told them that it was a good means of focusing their growing minds and controlling their imaginations.

Em picked up one of the tiny monks that Matt had taken such care in painting and turned it over in her hand. It had been rendered in fine detail, down to the tiny symbol of the monastic order of Era Mina on the back of the monk's robe.

A geometric shape like a swirling helix.

A crowd of thoughts pounded into Em, all at once. The helix. The mysterious figure that had haunted her in the night. He was connected to the abbey.

She held the proof in her hand.

The identity of the mysterious figure, haunting her. He was Albion.

TWENTY-ONE

Auchinmurn Isle
The Middle Ages

The sun dipped behind the horizon. The wind howled across the bay. Matt's clothes were damp against his skin, and his body ached from exhaustion. Worse, his stomach was rumbling furiously. He couldn't remember the last time he'd eaten. He dug his fingers into the corner of his coat pockets in the hope of something, but there wasn't even a fuzzy mint.

They were heading silently northwest toward the more rugged, uninhabited part of Auchinmurn. Solon was in the lead, his tunic singed and torn. Carik followed, holding her wounded hand close to her chest. Matt brought up the rear.

Matt was astonished at how much Auchinmurn had changed over the centuries. He had adapted to the overwhelming stink that permeated everything—a heady mix of burning peat, cooking pig fat, human waste, and animal manure, all punctuated with the sour smells of sweat. And unlike in the twenty-first century, the island's forest reached all the way to the shoreline, giving them cover as they climbed to the caves high up in the hillside.

Solon stopped under a cluster of pine trees. "Can you climb this, Matt?"

Matt looked up at the dense, overgrown cliff face in front of them, and nodded.

With Solon hacking through the heavy wet brush with his sword and Carik in the middle, Matt climbed slowly up the cliff behind them. Mud and water were still flowing through the bracken on this part of the island, so their ascent was a slippery one. Because of her swollen, blistered hand, Carik fell backward twice onto Matt. Her mistrust and wariness of him was still strong; he sensed it every time he set her back on her feet. He did his best to respond neutrally, but it wasn't easy. She and Solon both smelled sour, like burning wood tinged with rotting meat. It was hard not to wrinkle his nose and convey the wrong impression of his own feelings toward them both.

You hardly smell of scented soap, he reminded himself. The phrase was Jeannie's, and the memory caught in his throat. He hoped his dad's lifelong relationship with the old housekeeper was keeping him from harming her.

As they climbed, Matt wondered what was on this part of the

island in the present day. He, Em, and Zach knew all the coves and caves near Seaport and on Era Mina, but he didn't think Auchinmurn's spelunkers were aware of smugglers' caves on this side of the island.

An avalanche of rocks and roots tumbled toward Matt without warning.

"Look out!" Solon yelled, flattening himself against the crags.

Matt covered his head with his hands as rocks rained down on him, battering and cutting him. Curled against the rock face, he experienced a jolt of homesickness that took his breath away.

Carik reached out her good hand to Matt as the avalanche trickled to a halt. "You will see your sister again soon," she said.

Kindness at last, Matt thought wryly. She had obviously sensed his longing.

"I'm fine," he said shortly. "Keep going."

They climbed on in silence. Solon was some way ahead now, almost at the ridge line.

"Why did your father send those knights to attack us?" Carik asked abruptly.

Matt focused on where he was placing his hands. "I don't know. Maybe he didn't want us following him, seeing where he took Jeannie."

The higher they climbed, the thicker the bracken and brambles became. The moon was full now, glittering on the bay below them. Matt's hands and face were covered in scratches.

Above them, Solon had stopped at a thick curtain of bramble and hawthorn bushes, and Matt detected a cave opening behind their swinging branches.

"May I use your magic glasses again?" Solon asked.

Matt handed the opera glasses over. They huddled together on the ledge as Solon pressed the glasses to his eyes, focusing on the small island of Era Mina.

"What are you looking at?" asked Matt.

Solon returned the glasses to Matt. "Brother Renard's tower on Era Mina. The one we are building to keep him safe from his own fracturing imagination. Look."

The tower on Era Mina stood full height in Matt's time, slender and commanding. Right now it was partway through the process of being built.

The rocky promontory was swarming with hundreds of black knights in identical armor, cutting stone, mixing mortar, carrying bricks—building the tower at record speed and all moving in the same precise way Matt, Solon, and Carik had witnessed earlier on the beach. Matt wondered again at how his father was doing all of this. Guardians could not animate. What *were* these creatures? Where had they come from?

Solon took the glasses again. "Why does your father not animate the tower itself?"

"He's a Guardian," said Matt. "Not an Animare."

Solon looked startled. "Then how is he doing this?"

"I have no idea."

They moved inside the cave and Solon dropped the brush cover, plunging them into darkness. Matt could feel and smell Carik standing next to him. The sense of her mistrust and intense curiosity assailed him.

Who are you? she was saying, as clearly as if she were speaking the words aloud.

Matt wasn't sure he knew the answer to that either.

TWENTY-TWO

Solon crouched over a scratched-out fire pit with two sharp pieces of flint. In seconds, a fire burst to life in the center of the cave, illuminating the damp space. Then he loosened his sword and slumped onto a flat rock next to the fire.

Carik set her quiver, her bow, and a hunting knife on a flat rock that jutted out from the far wall like a tongue. She cupped her hand under the water that was trickling down the cave wall and mixed a poultice of moss, mud, and a powder she took from a pouch under her tunic before caking the mixture liberally on her blistered hand.

As Solon tossed more kindling on the fire, thick gray smoke rapidly filled the small cave. Matt started to cough, doing his best to clear the haze building up around him.

Solon grinned. "All will be well, Matt. Be patient."

He ducked to the corner of the cave and retrieved a tube made from a hollowed-out branch and coated on the inside with a black tar that glimmered in the firelight. Placed over the fire, the branch created a chimney that carried the smoke up and away, forcing it out through small fissures in the rock.

When the fire was blazing and the smoke under control, Solon pulled a leather pouch from his vest. Like Carik's, the pouch was full of dried plants and herbs. He broke off a chunk of what looked to Matt like a gingerroot and handed it to him. "This will help dull the pain in your head."

Matt was about to chew the root up when Solon slapped it from his hand. It landed, popping and sparking, in the fire.

"It is to be put on your *wound!*" said Solon, shaking his head in disbelief.

Carik burst out laughing at Matt's ignorance. Matt couldn't help himself and began to laugh too. He took another slice of the root. This time he did as instructed. Minutes after applying the gooey substance from the inside of the root, he felt the deep cut on his forehead slowly go numb.

"What happened to the white peryton?" he asked at last, getting as close to the fire as possible without burning himself. He was soaking wet and freezing cold, and every bone felt bruised from being tossed around in the raft. "The last I saw of her, you two were flying her over the wave."

"She brought us to safety above the waterline, and vanished," said Solon. "I'm not sure where she goes, deep into the island somewhere. Brother Renard and I unbound her from the island, to help save the village from the Norse attack."

"The Norsemen who attacked the monastery," said Matt, turning to Carik, who was gathering more wood at the mouth of the cave. "Were they your people? Vikings?"

Carik still wasn't doing a very good job at stifling her curiosity. Like the damp of the cave and the stink of their bodies, it continued washing over Matt in waves.

"They were not my people," she said fiercely. "I was their slave. They took my mother as spoils of one of their victories after they conquered the islands north of Skye, when I was still at her breast."

She tossed the wood into the fire, causing sparks to explode near Matt's feet. He jumped back.

"We need to find where your father has imprisoned my master, Brother Renard," said Solon.

"And where he's taken Jeannie," added Matt.

"Who exactly is this Jeannie?" asked Carik.

"She's our—"

Matt stopped, not sure of how to explain who Jeannie was, and what she meant to him and everyone at the abbey. He wasn't entirely sure who she was now anyway. Not after everything that had happened that day.

"She was the one who created the wave," he said finally. "She's from my time, in the future. I think she is connected to the islands in some enchanted way. Maybe like the peryton is."

Solon studied the fire. "We saw the destruction of the wave from the peryton. It surged through the monastery walls and destroyed the outer buildings, including our scriptorium." A shadow passed over his face. "Many manuscripts will have been destroyed."

Matt could only guess at how long a single manuscript would have taken these monks to illuminate. One more thing to feel guilty about.

A thought struck him.

"Solon," he said suddenly, "was *The Book of Beasts* kept in the scriptorium?"

Solon's gaze was suddenly as hard as a diamond.

"What do you know of that manuscript?" he asked warily.

If Matt was going to find and free Jeannie, let alone have any chance of returning to the twenty-first century, he would need Solon's help. Perhaps the help of the old monk Renard, too. He'd have to trust them with what he knew about *The Book of Beasts*.

But where to begin?

"My mum found a page to an ancient manuscript," he began. "*The Book of Beasts*. My sister and I googled it and learned how it had been used in the ninetieth century to open Hollow Earth—"

Matt paused. He could tell from Solon's expression that he'd lost him at "googled." He began again.

"My mum found evidence of the book's existence at the Royal Academy, in London."

"A royal academy?" Solon asked curiously. "For a king?"

Not for the first time in recent days, Matt wished he'd paid more attention to history.

"Kind of," he mumbled, deciding to fudge this bit. "She was a visitor to this academy and she found a page that proved the existence of a place called Hollow Earth. A place where Animare trapped the beasts and monsters from ancient times by drawing them into this manuscript, *The Book of Beasts*."

Solon's eyes sharpened in recognition. "My master, Brother Renard, told me a story right before your father arrived on the island. It was about the First Animare, Albion."

"You mentioned him earlier," said Matt.

Solon nodded. "Albion founded the monastery of Era Mina. He drew the first pages of *The Book of Beasts*. The mission of the monks since his death has been to continue this work, drawing the creatures into this manuscript and protecting their hiding place. The abbot told me that when *The Book of Beasts* is completed, it will seal Hollow Earth forever."

"Yes!" Matt exclaimed, drinking in this fresh information. "That's it exactly! Where is it now?"

"The abbot took it from my master when Brother Renard's mind began to break," said Solon. "For safekeeping. It may yet have escaped the wave."

"It's not complete yet, is it?" said Matt.

Solon shook his head. "There is one last beast to be sealed into Hollow Earth. The grendel. It lives in the swamp near the Devil's Dyke. Until it is drawn into the manuscript by a trained

Animare like my master, Brother Renard, Hollow Earth cannot be sealed. It is vulnerable to men like your father. We must finish it, but . . ." Solon lifted his hands hopelessly. "My master's mind is too fragile for such work now."

Carik had crawled outside and was now returning with her hands full of seeds, nuts, and one or two squirming wormy creatures that made Matt's stomach lurch despite his hunger. She handed each of the boys a handful of what she'd foraged.

"These I can eat, right?" Matt said weakly, trying not to look at what was in his hands.

Solon laughed and nodded. Matt tossed the whole lot into his mouth, chewed quickly, and tried to ignore the tickling in his throat as he swallowed. Carik crouched next to the fire, warming her hands, eating more slowly.

"We need to get into the abbot's tower in the monastery," said Solon, tearing the legs off a beetle before popping it in his mouth. "If the abbot had it before your father took him captive, he may have hidden it in his chambers."

Carik winced visibly as she rolled out a straw mat next to the fire. Noticing, Solon scooped two fingers into the root he had used to numb Matt's head wound.

"Show me your injury, Carik," he said gently.

Carik pulled her tunic off her shoulder and turned her back to the fire, revealing a hole the size of a fist directly under her shoulder blade. Matt gawked at the thin translucent skin healing over the center of the wound, barely concealing a pulsing hole in the girl's flesh. The edges of the wound had been cauterized, the flesh puckered and pink around the hole. But the hole itself looked like no wound Matt had ever seen before. It wasn't a bite, for there were no teeth marks. It wasn't a tear, for there were no claw marks. It was a wound that appeared to be breathing on its own.

Carik let Solon apply the syrup to the membrane covering the wound and tug her tunic gently back into place.

"What did that?" asked Matt uneasily.

"It is the mark of the grendel," said Carik. "I was lucky my courage abandoned me. If I hadn't turned my back to run, it would have sucked out my heart."

TWENTY-THREE

Outside the abbey, the perimeter lights came on. Simon's animation shield crisscrossed the top of the wall like a laser game of cat's cradle. Vaughn stood at the windows and watched the light show for a few minutes.

"What if Henrietta stole the tapestry because of what it showed?" he said.

"What makes you say that?" asked Renard.

"When Sir Charles finally broke into the Council room, he said he could still sense Henrietta's presence. Her emotions were so strong that they lingered." Vaughn paused. "He sensed joy and an overwhelming wave of triumph. I think we have to ask ourselves what happened in that room with the tapestry that could have caused such heightened emotions in Henrietta."

Renard shook his head. "Only one thing would elicit a response like that. A different outcome to the battle of Era Mina."

Em tried not to absorb too much of the fear and tension in the room; it was giving her a headache. "What was the battle of Era Mina?"

"We've always believed it depicted the story of the grendel attacking the monastery," said Renard. He looked older than Em had ever seen him. "But like so many of the stories about Hollow Earth, separating myth from reality is difficult."

The room grew cold. Em shivered.

Stay calm, Em. Zach reached his hand across to soothe her.

"Is the grendel . . . really bad?" she managed.

"He is a sin-eater, a beast that sucks out your soul and devours your body," said Vaughn grimly. "The original tapestry was woven by the monks in the mid–thirteenth century. It showed an army fighting the grendel, led by a shadowy figure in a cowled robe."

Simon jumped in. "The story we learned in school was that the grendel was finally stopped by a powerful monk who lured it back to the center of the earth—"

"To Hollow Earth?" Em interrupted.

"Yes," answered Simon.

"I think whatever else changed in the tapestry," said Vaughn, "the figure might now be Malcolm."

Sandie gave a disbelieving laugh. "How is that possible? That tapestry has hung in the Chamber of the Council of Guardians for centuries."

"Henrietta believes the figure is Malcolm, whether that's possible or not," said Vaughn. "In her mind Malcolm has changed history, which has changed the story of the tapestry."

"But why would she steal it?" Simon asked.

"This is only a guess," said Vaughn, "but I think that when she was waiting for her meeting with Sir Charles in the Council chambers, she saw the tapestry alter in some way. Maybe the face under the cowl became visible. Maybe the whole battle scene changed. She didn't want anyone else to see what had taken place, so she took the tapestry. There's your motivation."

Simon rubbed his hands over his face. "If Malcolm takes control of Hollow Earth, he will reset the Dark Ages. The monsters of old will return. This world has enough monsters of its own. It doesn't need any more."

"We will have no way of knowing whether Malcolm has succeeded in unlocking the beasts until it happens," said Vaughn. "We'll simply wake up in a world we no longer recognize."

"If that happens," signed Zach to his dad, "what will happen to us?"

"It's likely that Animare would be exposed to the public," said Simon. "Because they may be the only ones with the power to battle whatever is released upon the earth."

An eerie light flooded the kitchen.

"What the—" began Simon, startled.

Vaughn was already out of his chair and dashing through the French window. The others followed, running down the wide back lawn toward the jetty and the bay, staring in disbelief at Era Mina across the water.

Thick bands of light were spiraling around the peak of the small island. Inside each of the rings was a series of translucent orbs, like tiny moons. And inside each of the orbs was a twitching, writhing, scratching, screaming beast.

These were not holograms projected from somewhere on Era Mina. These were real animations. Em recognized a griffin, a gorgon, and hellhounds spinning next to a basilisk, a wraith, and a monstrous kraken.

The rings looked like an immense gyroscope, the orbs rotating faster and faster on their own axes. They were creating a chilling wind, flecking whitecaps on the bay, until Em could no longer distinguish any single creature inside the orbs.

"It looks like Era Mina is going to be pulled right out of the water!" she gasped.

"Is this it?" Sandie asked breathlessly. "Are we too late?"

As if someone switched off gravity, the bands suddenly slowed their rotation and fell away, the orbs dropping back into the island like falling stars.

"What the hell just happened, Renard?" Vaughn demanded.

"I have never seen anything like it before," said Renard, sounding shocked. "But I have heard of it. For as long as *The Book of Beasts* remains incomplete, the island and the creatures it protects are unstable. When the protectors of Hollow Earth are in mortal danger, the island reacts. Shifts. Threatens to break apart."

Simon looked ashen-faced. "I think it's safe to say that Jeannie is in trouble."

And not just Jeannie, Em thought numbly. *Matt as well.*

"How did we get here?" she heard her mother sob against Vaughn's jacket. "How did the promise of our future become such a curse? Jeannie . . . and Matt! How can he fight his dad by himself? He's thirteen years old!"

Renard and Simon slowly made their way back up the garden to the kitchen as Vaughn murmured soothing words and stroked Sandie's hair. She looked up at Vaughn, tears streaking her cheeks.

"Vaughn, do you ever think about how our lives would be if . . ."

Catching Em's eye, Sandie faltered to a guilty halt.

"It's okay, Mum," Em said as normally as she could. "I think about it all the time. What if you'd married Vaughn instead of Dad."

Sandie looked mortified. "Em, my love, I never meant—"

Em could feel her mother's anguish. It was almost unbearable.

"Really," she said more gently. "It's okay."

TWENTY-FOUR

FOURTEEN YEARS EARLIER

S itting at his desk in the abbey, Vaughn read the memo carefully.

"Anything good?" asked Malcolm, lolling in the doorway.

Vaughn looked up. "Does the name Wyeth Corcoran mean anything to you?"

Malcolm twirled a pencil between his fingers. "Wyeth Corcoran . . . the Animare illustrator? He does kids' books, something like that."

Vaughn nodded. He studied the memo again. "He died this morning."

"Too bad."

Malcolm sounded uninterested, still flipping his pencil between his fingers, as if Wyeth Corcoran's death was the least interesting thing he had heard all day. Malcolm Calder was a brilliant Guardian, and Vaughn knew he was lucky to have him as his partner, but empathy had never been Malcolm's strong suit. It was a failing in someone who dealt in emotions.

"What does his death have to do with Orion?" Malcolm finally asked.

"While drawing his last breath, Wyeth Corcoran created a death animation."

At last a spark of interest showed in Malcolm's blue eyes. "Unusual, but not unheard of. Do they need us to eliminate it?"

Vaughn nodded. "It's been at his place for several hours. Alice Macnair, Corcoran's Guardian, has been trying to destroy it, but she's too old and grief stricken at the loss of Wyeth and it's beyond her."

"No one else has seen it?" Malcolm asked.

"If they have, I'm sure Alice followed protocol and managed to convince them it was a ghost." Vaughn checked the memo again. "Wyeth lived on the Isle of Arran. We've got the assignment to dispatch the animation because we're the closest agents in the vicinity. Let's go."

They made the short drive south along the Ayrshire coast to Ardrossan, where they picked up the car ferry across the Firth of Clyde to Arran. The day was sunny but cool for July, a brisk north wind keeping their collars up and their heads down.

From the upper deck of the ferry Vaughn watched the peak of Goat Fell rise to greet them. Midway across the Firth, Malcolm leaned close.

"I have news."

Vaughn wasn't sure he liked the smile on his Guardian's face. "Tell," he said warily.

"Sandie's pregnant."

Vaughn felt sick. He was pretty sure the nausea he was suddenly feeling had nothing to do with the rough motion of the boat.

"You're not serious," he said at last. "Malcolm, do you have any idea how many rules you've just broken? A Guardian and an Animare can't have kids!"

Malcolm sighed. "You know your trouble? You worry too much."

Vaughn couldn't believe how calm Malcolm was. "The combination of Animare and Guardian powers in children is forbidden, and with good reason! What were you *thinking?*"

Malcolm laughed and slapped Vaughn's back. "Don't worry so much . . ."

Vaughn pulled away. "This isn't a joke, Malcolm. You and Sandie will be ostracized. Your child will be persecuted. You're a stupid, reckless fool and now your selfishness, your narcissism, your blatant disregard for the Council's authority has put Sandie's future in jeopardy and I—"

"*I'm* a fool?" interrupted Malcolm. "What about you? You've been pining for Sandie since university, and you never acted on your feelings. Not once."

Vaughn bit his tongue and turned into the wind, away from

this man who he was meant to be as close to as any two people could be. Not for the first time, he wished he'd spoken up about Malcolm and Sandie's forbidden relationship from the start, instead of promising Malcolm that he would keep it a secret. Since university, their bond as Animare and Guardian had been festering with conflict, not simply from Vaughn's jealousy over Malcolm and Sandie's relationship, but also from Malcolm's brooding envy of Vaughn's abilities as an Animare—especially when Vaughn refused to break or bend any of the rules.

Sea spray stung Vaughn's eyes. He wiped his tears with his sleeve.

Resting his forearms on the rail, Malcolm stared across at Arran's mountainous terrain. "You're worse than a fool, V," he said. "You're a romantic with a code far too chivalrous for your own good. You'd have been happier in a world where we would joust for our fair maiden's hand."

"Instead of a world where you use your . . . your . . ." Vaughn exhaled slowly, letting the wind carry his bitterness and the rest of his words.

"Say it!" said Malcolm, stabbing the air in front of Vaughn's chest. "Your suspicions are choking you. I can feel them."

Vaughn glared at Malcolm, in his Ramones T-shirt and his army surplus jacket, his hair wild and unkempt, looking every inch the struggling rock star. The men were physically matched in height, but Vaughn had muscle on Malcolm, who was rake thin.

Vaughn refused to give Malcolm the satisfaction of a brawl.

He shoved past his Guardian and took the narrow metal steps down to the main deck two at a time.

"Say it," Malcolm yelled after him. "You think I inspirited Sandie! That I'm some kind of mad Merlin! You can't stand it that she simply fell in love with me!"

Neither man spoke again until they pulled off Arran's beach road onto a grassy shoulder in front of Wyeth Corcoran's renovated eighteenth-century gatehouse.

"I've heard about this place," said Malcolm as if nothing had happened on the ferry at all. "Wyeth gutted it to make it accessible for his wheelchair. Won some awards."

The tall two-story structure had once been the gatehouse to Lochranza Castle, whose ruins sat directly across a watery inlet that, centuries ago, had been a natural moat. Arched windows stretched from the second floor to the turreted roof, reflecting the midday sun off the firth and bathing everything in a silvery sheen, including a jagged rock with a seal basking in the warmth.

A frail but chipper woman gripping a cane to steady herself against the buffeting wind was waiting for them at the gate.

Alice Macnair's eyes were red and watery. "The animation's inside," she said, twisting her cane between her hands. "I managed to contain it in Wyeth's study. I could nae take care of it on my own. These legs aren't what they used to be. And I couldn't chance that I'd fail. It would be quite a shock for auld Doc Ernst when he shows up tae find me dead too."

Malcolm sauntered toward the front door ahead of Vaughn

and Alice, the air filled with the sickly sweet perfume from the hedgerows of pink roses bordering the path. Vaughn's stomach pitched again. If he and Malcolm had any chance of surviving as a team, they had to get through this. Rage assailed him again as he thought of the impossible position Malcolm had put Sandie in.

Stepping into the gatehouse was like stepping into the pages of a sword-and-sorcery picture book. The walls were a solid mural depicting scenes from classic stories, one bleeding into the other. Sir Walter Scott's Lady Rowena on her tournament throne next to Prince Caspian on a dressage horse galloping toward the Lady of the Lake offering the sword to King Arthur. The most spectacular part of the mural showed King Richard the Lionheart, broadsword drawn, fighting a double-winged dragon whose tail Wyeth had painted around the banister that climbed the room beside the specially constructed wheelchair ramp to the first-floor balcony, creating the illusion that the beast had sprung from the balcony itself. Windows flooded the space with light that spilled onto the images and made them even more realistic.

Vaughn had helped Alice to a chair near the galley kitchen when a high-pitched, blood-curdling scream shook the entire house. The sound of a mallet on thick wood followed. *Thump! Thump! Thump!* And then the feral scream began again, rising to a screeching crescendo before it stopped, leaving the thumping to fill the barbed silence once more.

"That's Wyeth's study. His bedroom is just beyond it," said Alice, nodding at the ground-level door beside the kitchen.

The screeching and the thumping began again.

Malcolm looked at Vaughn. "Let's get this done before my ears explode."

The screaming grew even louder, a squawking, tortured screech. The heavy thumping had the rhythm of large, uneven footsteps.

As the men cautiously approached the door, a chill of briny, fetid air swirled through the lock, seeping around the wooden edges like a damp fog. A cold hand touched Vaughn's as he prepared to turn the handle. He jumped.

Alice was standing next to him. "You may need this," she said, handing him a birdcage the size of a suitcase.

"What exactly was the old man working on when he died?" asked Malcolm warily.

"A pop-up edition of *Treasure Island*."

TWENTY-FIVE

Dispatching the death animation didn't take long. Vaughn was swabbing up the puddles of watercolors on the floor of the bedroom when Alice showed the doctor and the undertakers into the room to deal with the old man's body.

"A fine way to go, working on a picture like this," said the doctor, admiring the image of Long John Silver and his rambunctious parrot on Wyeth Corcoran's easel. "It's what he would have wanted."

"Thank you for your help," said Alice, looking gratefully at Vaughn as the undertakers started to prepare the old man's body. "Have you far to go home?"

"Just across the firth," said Vaughn. "We'll wait with you until Wyeth leaves. Won't we, Malcolm?"

JOHN BARROWMAN & CAROLE E. BARROWMAN

Malcolm was prowling around the room, turning over papers, poking inside drawers, as if neither Alice Macnair nor Vaughn were in the room.

Wyeth Corcoran's shelves were as choked with collectibles as his walls were with art. What wasn't part of a mural was hanging from picture rails or leaning against shelves, beside furniture, even in the spaces between books on the bookshelves. Unframed canvases competed with exquisitely framed ones for open space. Vaughn saw the works of minor Scottish artists and a few masters and other pieces he recognized as sketches of Wyeth Corcoran's most famous book covers.

"Bit of a mess this, isn't it?" Malcolm remarked, looking around.

The events of the day were taking their toll on the elderly Guardian. Her hands trembled when she accepted a gingersnap from Vaughn, who had found a tin in the kitchen. "Wyeth collected anything wi' a connection to the western isles," she said. "He has left most of this collection in his will to the Scottish National Gallery. A few favorites he's given to me."

Vaughn noticed that she kept her eyes on Malcolm, who had shifted his attentions to an open jewelry box beside a locked display cabinet that hung beneath the painted curve of the dragon's belly on the wall.

The old Guardian stiffened in her seat as Malcolm peered closer into the cabinet.

"This is an interesting artifact," said Malcolm conversationally. He tapped the glass, pointing at a dull golden medallion within. "What's its provenance, Alice?"

"I believe it belonged to Wyeth's sister," answered Alice in guarded tones.

Malcolm's blue eyes were calculating. "You've really no further information?"

Alice jumped to her feet as the undertakers carried the coffin from the bedroom on their broad shoulders, knocking her cup and saucer to the floor. "Oh my goodness," she said, as if her clumsiness had startled her.

Vaughn moved to help her, but she waved him away and knelt down to pick up the pieces. So instead he followed the coffin outside, helped raise it onto the back of the hearse, and waited until he saw it safely on its way along the beach road before he stepped back inside.

The main room was empty. The glass case was unlocked. No Alice. No Malcolm.

A horrible scream filled the vast room, full of anguish and most certainly human. Vaughn looked up in shock at the balcony. Alice was splayed on the floor with Malcolm looming over her, his hands gripping her shoulders.

Vaughn sprinted up the ramp, barreling into Malcolm. The impact sent Malcolm flying backward, crashing through the wooden rails and out over the edge of the balcony. Reacting in an instant, Malcolm grabbed at the carpet, stopping his fall but leaving him dangling dangerously high above the stone floor.

"Hey!" he shouted, struggling. "Hey, get me up!"

Ignoring Malcolm's cries, Vaughn knelt next to Alice and checked her pulse. It was strong, but one of her ears was bleeding, the blood trickling down her pale neck.

On the other side of the broken rail Malcolm was trying to haul himself up, swinging his legs like a pendulum. His momentum caused the carpet to tear from its mooring, dropping him farther. Vaughn stomped on the runner, slowing Malcolm's descent.

"No. No," Alice groaned.

Vaughn realized with disgust that Malcolm had inspirited the old Guardian to the point of suffering. Enraged, he took his foot off the runner again. The carpet slipped farther. Malcolm howled.

"What did you do to her?" demanded Vaughn, stepping back onto the carpet.

"She was lying to me about that medallion!" Malcolm's exertion was reddening his face as he swung, frantically trying to keep a grip. "How was I to know how frail her mind was?"

"By *looking* at her!" Vaughn roared.

The carpet gave up, sliding away completely from under Vaughn's foot. For a beat Malcolm bicycled in the air, grasping at the shifting rug for traction. Vaughn shot out his arm and grabbed Malcolm's hand. Wordlessly he dragged his Guardian's upper body onto the balcony, leaving him to scramble up the rest of the way on his own.

TWENTY-SIX

Vaughn set the unconscious Alice gently on a daybed on the balcony. Holding a corner of his T-shirt to the cut above his eye, Malcolm slowly stood up and went down the ramp.

Alice's eyes fluttered open.

"What happened?" asked Vaughn.

She opened her fist.

The medallion from the locked cabinet looked a lot like the coins the Guardian Council used for secret votes, until Vaughn looked closer. Instead of a white stag on the front of the coin—the symbol for Animare—and the helix indicating Guardians on the reverse side, this medallion had an inverted spiral with its point on the top. On the reverse side was the image of a black peryton with a flaming saddle.

Vaughn pressed the coin back into Alice's hands. "What is this?"

"Have ye ever heard of Hollow Earth?"

"Of course. It's one of our myths, part of our creation story." Vaughn smiled and squeezed her hand. Had Malcolm rattled her more deeply than he thought? "It's a story, Alice," he went on gently. "No one believes in Hollow Earth's existence anymore."

"Wyeth did." She nodded feebly down toward the kitchen, where Malcolm was noisily opening and closing cupboards. "And he believes it too."

"Malcolm?" Vaughn said disbelievingly.

"Yes. He wanted to know about the Hollow Earth Society."

Vaughn tried to keep hold of the conversation. "The Hollow Earth *Society*? Who are they?"

Alice gazed steadily at him. "A secret organization who believes that Hollow Earth must be protected at all costs. An organization Wyeth's sister belonged to."

Someone believed Hollow Earth was real? Not just real but worth protecting? "Protected from whom?" Vaughn said at last.

"Wyeth's sister and several others believed that someone of immense power had started up a rebel faction inside the society." Alice's voice was growing weaker. She rolled the coin in her hand. "This faction wasn't interested in protecting Hollow Earth. They wanted to open it, and use the beasts for their own purposes. Wyeth's sister said that this coin was a way of identifying those rebels." She lay back against the pillows, exhausted.

"Go, son. I'll be fine. I promise. Go and leave me to my grief. You've enough of your own coming your way."

She drifted away into a deep sleep, the kind Vaughn knew came from a powerful inspiriting. The balcony was cold; she needed a pillow and blanket to keep her comfortable.

Vaughn went downstairs, hunting for the linen closet. When he found it next to Wyeth's bedroom, he grabbed a pillow and a blanket and carried them back up the ramp to Alice. Lifting her softly snoring head, he slipped the pillow underneath and draped the blanket across her frail legs.

Her hand was open and the coin was gone.

Vaughn sprinted outside just as Malcolm and the Land Rover disappeared around the curve of the island.

It was a long trek on foot to the ferry.

Vaughn returned to the abbey, packed up his belongings, and left. He couldn't stay anymore. Although his heart broke at leaving Sandie, he hoped never to see Malcolm again.

Two things haunted him as he took his motorbike south. Who was the person with "immense power" that Alice mentioned leading the quest to control Hollow Earth? And—more pressingly—why had he saved Malcolm Calder's life?

TWENTY-SEVEN

E nough moping around," Renard said briskly, setting a brown leather satchel on the table. "We need a plan."

As Renard opened the satchel's catches, Em could see a handful of silver medallions inside, a stack of letters tied with twine, and the opening page from *The Book of Beasts* in its Plexiglas sleeve.

Renard took two coins from the bag and slid them across the table, one to Zach and one to Em. Em turned hers over in her hand, recognizing the white peryton on one side and the etching of the silver helix on the other. She thought about her ghostly visitor again.

Simon took over the conversation. "In our research we have discovered that the black and white perytons are the Protectors of these islands. They appear whenever a descendant of the First Animare, Albion, calls for help."

"So they're like the island's avatars?" signed Zach.

"Exactly." Simon picked up the coin in front of Zach. "We've always known that this peryton was a symbol of the Animare." He tapped the tiny peryton on the medallion. "Until recently, we always assumed that the etching on the back, the helix, was the Guardian symbol."

"And now?" asked Em, studying the silver helix on the back of her coin, rubbing her thumb over the etching.

"Now that we know the stories of Hollow Earth are in fact true," Simon continued, "we think the helix means something quite different."

"What?"

"It has always stood for the monastic Order of Era Mina, representing both Animare and Guardian," Renard said. "But now we think it has something to do with time. How we perceive it, how we measure it. The shape suggests time is not linear, as we generally perceive it to be—one event after another, creating ripples of complex causes and effects, measured as seconds, then minutes, accumulating into hours and days and so on. We think this represents the fact that Hollow Earth exists outside the normal way we measure time. It is eternal."

A quote jolted into Em's mind.

To our sons and daughters. May you never forget imagination is the real and the eternal. This is Hollow Earth.

If time was a series of overlapping circles as Renard described, it was exactly like the great gyroscope of beasts they had just seen spinning over Era Mina. *Real and eternal*. If it was true, Hollow Earth existed *outside* time.

More understanding surged through Em. The quote had never been just about the place where the beasts of the ancient stories and myths had been imprisoned. It was also about those who must protect Hollow Earth with their imaginations. The sons and daughters of the island's first defenders, through all of time. Countless individuals down the generations. Renard and Jeannie.

Her and Matt.

"Years ago, Em," said Vaughn, pulling her attention back to the conversation, "your dad found a coin similar to these, but with a black peryton on the reverse. I think that discovery set him and his mother, Henrietta, on their quest to find and open Hollow Earth."

Simon passed two mugs of hot chocolate to Zach and Em. Em sipped the rich, creamy drink, letting it soothe her. Fresh ideas shifted and settled in her head.

"Do you know where Hollow Earth is, Grandpa?" she asked.

"It lies beneath and between the two islands, in a supernatural hollow at the center of the earth."

I knew it!

Zach arched his eyebrows at Em. *You did not.*

Renard slipped the page of *The Book of Beasts* in its Plexiglas cover out of the satchel. "In ancient times, the monks of Era Mina began this *Book of Beasts* to bind the beasts in Hollow Earth, lock them away forever. Albion is said to live there with them, guarding them. Only two direct descendants of Albion can open Hollow Earth again."

"One to use the sacred bone quill Dad stole from the monks to draw the beasts out again," Em guessed. "And the other to keep their emotions steady and controlled as they do it. Right?"

Renard nodded.

Sandie paled. "Malcolm is a Guardian descendant of Albion. He only needs *The Book of Beasts*, the bone quill, and an Animare?"

Vaughn swore loudly and got up from the table. Em jumped from her chair.

Take it easy, Em . . .

"Mum!" Em was barely able to hear Zach's voice through the drumming in her head. "Matt's the Animare! Dad already has the bone quill. If he finds *The Book of Beasts*, all he has to do is inspirit Matt to do what he wants. Then he'll have all he needs!"

PART TWO

TWENTY-EIGHT

T he setting sun dodged in and out of the clouds, raking light across Edinburgh Castle and the historic buildings of the city's Old Town. Henrietta de Court was enjoying high tea in the Balmoral Hotel on Princes Street, at a table with a clear view across the Royal Gardens to the National Gallery of Scotland, where, three hours ago, she had watched the handsome and enigmatic Orion agent Vaughn Grant sprint from the gallery, tear up the stack of parking tickets stuck to his motorcycle, and roar west toward the motorway.

She expected he would go directly to the abbey before he began tracking her and the tapestry, which at the moment was securely stored in an old cottage she had taken on Auchinmurn.

The morning's euphoria had left her feeling dangerously giddy.

Henrietta was not a woman to laugh lightly, but she smiled now, affording herself the luxury of humor. Although not quite as she had intended, this would be the catalyst for her coup, her seizure of full authority in the Council of Guardians, first in Europe and then across the rest of the world. She had confidants and collaborators in place, ready to move with speed and aggression at her command, the moment she gave it.

She signaled for the waiter with a sharp snap of her fingers.

"More tea," she instructed. "And two additional place settings. I am expecting company."

The waiter hurried away to do her bidding. Nibbling on a ladyfinger, Henrietta recalled how she had first doubted her son when he suggested his plan to her years ago. Malcolm's vision for the Councils was brilliant, and with her contacts and abilities she knew they would be unstoppable. It was almost unforgivable that she had let Renard's weak character influence her view of her son and for that she was truly sorry. When he was a child, Henrietta had worried that Malcolm would grow up to be like his father, lacking any ambition beyond the world of the islands and the limits of the rules. Certainly Renard never had any inclination that Sandie was a mere pawn in their plan for power. She doubted that he was aware of her part in all of this, even today.

The waiter set two places opposite Henrietta, then exchanged her tea for a fresh pot. She spread strawberry jam on a warm scone, added a dollop of fresh cream, and bit into its sweet softness, catching a drop of jam oozing onto her chin with her little finger. Outside, the evening traffic was clogging Princes Street. Her guests were late.

"*Seul le coeur sait ce que le coeur veut.*" It was a favorite expression of Henrietta's mother. "The heart knows what the heart wants." Despite the competition from the brooding Vaughn, Sandie had indeed fallen deeply in love with Malcolm. It had made their plan for a union between an Animare and a Guardian almost too easy. And for that union to result in twins, and such powerful ones at that—*ca c'etait la cerise sur le gâteau!* The cherry on the cake.

Of course there had been setbacks over the years—Malcolm's sudden disappearance the worst one of all. It was a betrayal Henrietta had finally coaxed out of Sir Charles, the conniving mercenary fool. Binding Malcolm was a treachery Renard and Sandie would pay for.

The waiter led her guests to the table. Henrietta licked cream from her fingers and carefully wiped her hands on her napkin before standing and greeting her fellow conspirators.

"It is not the way we had planned for our coup to begin," she said, picking up the silver teapot and filling her guests' cups, "but the time has finally come."

"A toast?" inquired the handsome, green-eyed man.

"How delicious," said his beautiful, dark-haired friend.

"To our sons and daughters," said the man, nodding at Henrietta as he raised his cup.

"Never forget imagination is the real and the eternal," purred the woman, pushing her long ink-black hair away from her face.

Henrietta smiled at Mara and Tanan and added the final line with flair.

"This is Hollow Earth."

TWENTY-NINE

In your time, Matt, are our kind worshipped?" asked Carik, stretching her legs out in front of the fire.

"The opposite," replied Matt. "We must keep ourselves hidden."

"Then time has not changed much at all," she said, pulling off her calfskin boots and drying her feet at the fire.

Carik was right, Matt realized. For all the progress and the developments that human beings had managed to achieve, they still hadn't figured out how to handle people who were different.

There was an odd rumbling sound.

"I'm hungry," Matt said defensively as Solon and Carik looked at him. "It's been a while since I ate."

Carik pulled her boots back on and lifted her bow from the rock behind her to look for more food. Solon followed her to the mouth of the cave. Matt concentrated on stabbing at the fire while doing his best to eavesdrop on their conversation.

"Go to the north from here, Carik. You'll be safer away from the monastery and the monks. Matt's father is growing more powerful every minute. I can feel it."

"Will you be safe, Solon?"

Matt sensed Solon glancing back at him. He concentrated on tossing another log on the fire.

"I will be fine."

Carik ducked out into the forest, leaving Matt and Solon alone at the fire.

"We probably could have animated a meal," said Matt into the silence.

Solon looked at him in horror. "We don't use our skills for the mundane and the ordinary."

"But it's who we are," said Matt, surprised at Solon's reaction.

"Our powers are a gift from nature, from the islands themselves." It was clear that Solon was offended. "To violate that gift would be dishonorable. A sin."

Matt rolled his eyes. "Sometimes you have to break rules in order to make things better for people."

"But what if, by breaking the rules, you cause more damage than leaving things the way they were?"

Matt thought about this. "I guess that's the chance you take.

When you break rules you have to be prepared to live with the consequences."

Solon prodded the fire. "Are you?"

"Am I what?"

"Prepared to live with the consequences of your actions? Of bringing your father to this time and place and the threat he represents to your future?"

Matt concentrated on the other Animare's emotions, teasing them out from the hunger and the exhaustion. The fire spat and crackled between them. He sensed concern and anxiety. No judgment. No quarrel with Matt or his choices. Poor though many of them had been.

"I'm prepared," said Matt.

Solon pulled his dagger from his sheath, offering it to Matt. "Then I will help you destroy him," he said simply. "I will help you defeat your father. Take this as a gesture of my allegiance."

The bronze hilt of Solon's dagger was etched like the wings of the white peryton. Turning the dagger over in his hands, Matt appreciated its weight. Then everything changed.

As if he were holding a tuning fork, Matt felt the dagger's reverberations ripple up his arm and across his shoulders as a cacophony of images exploded in his mind.

At first he couldn't distinguish or separate them from the conflagration of light and color. It was as if someone had edited a bunch of movie clips together and was running them all at once at superspeed in Matt's head.

One image stood out. Matt being dragged through a labyrinth of passageways and dark caves . . . and blood. Lots of it, leaving a trail behind him.

"It's . . . it's stunning . . . and, uh, heavy," said Matt, breathless and worried as the shock of the images quieted in his head.

"It belongs to my master, Brother Renard. He told me it was forged from the dark deposits of Hollow Earth, and it belonged to the Albion himself."

Matt had no idea what he had just sensed from the ancient dagger, but he knew it was showing him something of his future. Pressing the dagger back into Solon's hands, he looked directly at him.

"I need to talk to your master. Right now."

"I'm afraid," said Solon sadly, "that's not going to be easy."

THIRTY

Auchinmurn Isle

Present Day

Two days after Vaughn's return from London, things began to go missing from the abbey. Two cup-size iron bowls from Simon's prehistoric beaker collection. An altar triptych, depicting the Old Testament story of Daniel in the lion's den from the downstairs sitting room. Two framed maps of the island and an assortment of old books.

Worried that the abbey's perimeters had been breached by burglars, Vaughn had taken the boat out to check that the islands were secure. Simon planned to walk the perimeter of the abbey compound, to be sure that no one had broken through the animation shield.

"I can't understand it," said Renard in irritation, striding into the kitchen, his glasses on top of his head and holding his long white hair from his face. "I've lost that folder with the medieval maps I was examining in the library this morning. The one I found in the vault belonging to Duncan Fox. A bit tattered, black, ties with a leather strap?"

"Where did you have it last?" asked Em, sitting comfortably at the kitchen table, layering chutney onto her thick toasted-cheese sandwich.

She smiled across the table at Zach, who she knew was keeping a watchful eye on her. She'd have to explain soon to Zach what she was doing, but she needed to work a few things out on her own first. She owed that much to Matt . . . and to Jeannie.

"That folder was on my desk in the library this morning when I went down the driveway to fetch the mail," Renard said. "I swear it was."

He marched out through the French doors and onto the patio, where he met Simon coming out the gate from Jeannie's garden. Em watched them chat with some intensity for a few minutes. Simon shook his head and followed Renard back inside, ruffling Zach's hair as he walked past the table.

I hate it when he does that.

Aw, I think it's sweet. You're still his wee bairn.

Zach scowled at Em, who laughed and wolfed her lunch.

"We *need* those papers," said Renard, banging the kitchen table emphatically. "Duncan Fox is the only Animare in recent history to have witnessed the opening of Hollow Earth. He is the only person who can offer us any insights about what to expect if Malcolm has succeeded in his insane plan to do the same."

"Wouldn't it be easier to go back to 1848 and ask him ourselves?" said Em. "I know," she added hurriedly as Renard reddened with anger. "No time travel until we have a plan, but—"

"Emily Calder, *no buts!* We don't know enough about what time travel does to your mind, or to your body for that matter. We do it my way, or we don't do it at all!"

Em's eyes filled with tears. Her grandfather had never yelled at her like that before. Zach sat forward watchfully.

"I'm sorry, Em," Renard said in a more gentle tone. "I'm worried about Matt and Jeannie . . . and you."

He leaned over and drew her into a big hug. For a few beats Em felt safe and loved and as comforted as she had in ages. She desperately wanted to tell him that she had a plan, but she couldn't . . . not yet. She gave him a watery smile instead.

Renard pulled his glasses from his head and tapped them on the table. "Now," he said, "on with the hunt."

Em watched her grandfather head back to the library with a mug of tea in his hand. Her feelings were a confused mixture of anxiety and anger. She was pretty sure that Renard had just inspirited her, and quieted her emotions enough to sense that she was lying to him.

THIRTY-ONE

The folder refused to be found.

"Maybe you left it sitting on the mailbox when you fetched the mail, Renard," said Sandie, pouring Zach and Em glasses of milk. "I've done that before."

"Zach and I can walk down and check if you like," Em suggested.

She did her best to project an image in her mind of Jeannie making dumplings to protect her thoughts from Renard's penetrating gaze.

Renard turned to Simon. "Are you sure the compound hasn't been breached? I've been feeling strange since yesterday. Something's up, I can feel it." He rubbed the back of his neck.

"I'll walk the wall again and check for residual light from an animation," said Simon, "but you did only wake from your coma a couple of weeks ago. It's been a stressful few days."

"Have some lunch, Renard," said Sandie. "Think on a full stomach."

Renard sat at the counter and accepted his toasted cheese. "Ah, the lunch of kings," he said ironically.

"I'm doing my best," Sandie protested. "I thought I'd try Jeannie's chicken pesto recipe for dinner." She eyed Simon. "If Simon ever gets around to picking basil from the garden."

"No sooner said than done," said Simon, opening a kitchen drawer. He rummaged around for a few seconds, a frown forming on his face.. "That's weird," he said, coming out empty-handed. "Jeannie's garden scissors aren't in their usual place."

Em saw the garden scissors flash into her mind. She knew exactly where they were. She stood up from the table, tightening her concentration so as not to allow Renard access to her thoughts as she slowly and deliberately loaded her empty plate and glass into the dishwasher.

"Try the shed. Maybe she left them down there," said Renard.

"I doubt it," said Simon. "She really splurged to buy these. I can't see her leaving them in that damp old hut."

"I was in there this morning getting a rake . . . to clean up the beach," said Em quickly. "The only things in there are the mower and bags of potting soil."

Zach frowned at her. *When were you in Jeannie's shed? You hate being in there. It's full of spiders.*

Em had been ignoring Zach a lot lately. She felt bad about it, but she had to keep him out of her mind at the moment. She tried not to look at the hurt expression on his face.

Renard glanced suspiciously at them both. So did Simon.

"What's going on with you two?" said Sandie, looking at Em and Zach more closely. "You've been strange with each other all morning. Something we should know about?"

"Ask Em," Zach signed, shrugging.

"Nothing's going on!" Em protested, doing her best to avoid eye contact with Renard.

Renard raised his eyebrows. "I doubt that's the truth, but I won't press you."

What you don't know won't hurt you.

As soon as she thought it, Em knew from the look on Renard's face that she'd made a mistake.

"If we're going to figure out a plan to retrieve Matt and Jeannie from the Middle Ages before Malcolm uses one or both of them to access Hollow Earth," her grandfather said, looking sharply at her, "then we need to work *together*. And that means no more secrets."

Em could feel his accusation like a flashing neon light in her mind.

"Understood?"

Em nodded meekly.

"Me too," signed Zach.

Renard headed out to the foyer. He turned back at the door.

"Em and Zach, come to my study after you've checked the front gate for the folder. I believe we need to talk."

Em breathed a sigh of relief as her grandfather left. He was getting too close to the truth for comfort. She glanced at Zach, but he wouldn't look at her.

"Now this is really a bit much," said Sandie, making a lot of noise shifting dishes around in the cupboard above the stove. "I wanted to follow Jeannie's recipe to the letter and use her pestle and mortar to crush the garlic and pine nuts, and I can't find it."

"What's wrong with the food processor?" asked Simon.

"I thought I'd do it Jeannie's way," Sandie answered, her voice catching in her throat. "Without gadgets. Matt . . . Matt always loved it."

Em couldn't bear the sadness on her mother's face. Rushing across the kitchen, she hugged Sandie. "Matt and Jeannie are both going to be all right, Mum," she said. "I can feel it."

Sandie cupped Em's face in her hands. "I know," she said. "I'm just worried about them. But I have faith in Renard. He'll find a way to bring them both home safely." Dropping a kiss on Em's head, she moved back briskly to the stove. "Are you and Zach going to take a walk down the lane and check for that missing folder by the mailbox outside the gates? Simon will de-animate the shield for you."

THIRTY-TWO

The winding driveway snaked from the iron gate off Auchinmurn's main road to the abbey's massive oak door. Centuries
ago, the lane had been a camouflaged trail that pirates used for
smuggling their contraband inland from the island's hidden coves.
Now cultivated with low hedgerows and trimmed trees, its original stone-and-shell gravel tarred and smooth, the driveway was
the only access to the abbey other than from the sea or through
the dense woods north of the wall.

Up ahead shafts of sunlight filtered through the trees, creating long shadows across their path. Em watched them shift and
stretch as she walked, and was soon imagining the shadows peel-
ing themselves from the ground and rising up like tall tin soldiers
to lead the way.

The surface of the tar rippled in the sunlight. Em stopped, suddenly afraid of what the shadows might become.

Zach stared at her curiously. "You okay?"

A salty breeze rustled the trees, a cloud sliced across the sun, and the shadows vanished. Em exhaled slowly, relaxing her muscles and her mind. She was pleased that her lessons with Simon about controlling her imagination were paying off. The tall tin soldiers stayed inside her head, where they belonged.

"I thought I saw a deer," she signed to Zach, determined to keep her emotions in check and her conversation light.

Zach's anxiety for Matt made Em sad. Not the kind of sadness that she felt about Matt being gone—that felt as if a hole had opened in her heart, a hole that made her gasp for her breath at the oddest moments. But the kind of sadness that makes you want to cheer that person up, to make them smile, to help shake it off, to make their heart lighter.

"Do you want to race to the gate?" Em signed, nudging him with her elbow.

"Not really." He rolled an acorn in his hand, before tossing it into the air and kicking it into the surrounding trees. He stepped off the path and into the long grass to gather up more acorns.

What's going on with you, Em?

Em flinched. *Nothing.*

Don't lie to me.

I'm not.

Em could feel Zach's anger like a white heat behind her eyes.

Then, in an instant, it was gone. Instead, a pale blue light danced in Em's head. It curled like a silk ribbon around her thoughts.

I know you're keeping something from me.

Em had to distract him. Without thinking too hard about what she was about to do, she stepped up on her tiptoes and kissed Zach on the lips.

He backed away, his face flushed and full of confusion. "Why did you do that?"

Em shrugged, suddenly embarrassed. "I thought you might like it. I thought—"

"Well . . . well . . . I didn't!"

He marched on ahead, leaving Em with a pile of acorns at her feet. She picked one up and fired it at Zach, missing his head by centimeters.

Boys are stupid and annoying! I hate them!

Zach glared back at her before disappearing around a curve in the lane.

THIRTY-THREE

I feel bad about leaving Carik in the cave," said Matt, sitting behind Solon on the broad, gleaming back of the white peryton as it circled silently above the abbey in the darkness.

"You saw how her wound pains her and slows her down," said Solon. The peryton banked toward the monastery, its white wings as silent as clouds. "She needs to rest. If we are to find *The Book of Beasts* before your father does, we need to be quick. It's better for her to sleep."

"I still think we should rescue Jeannie and Brother Renard first," said Matt stubbornly.

"We need *The Book of Beasts* to bargain with," Solon pointed out. "We will look first in the abbot's tower, where I last saw the manuscript."

Thanks to Carik's hunting skills they had feasted on a fat rabbit earlier, and Matt always felt more amenable on a full stomach. "Fine," he grumbled. "I just hope you're right."

As the peryton glided over the tops of the trees, Matt saw the monastery's portcullis was secured. One of its animated hellhound guardians was prostrate near the gatehouse. Every few seconds, the hellhound's fiery breath flamed into the darkness.

Suddenly the massive hound leaped to its feet and into the center of the courtyard. It stopped and raised its burning snout into the air as if trailing the scent of sheep or cattle.

"Let's try to avoid that thing," said Matt, shivering.

Before Solon could nudge the peryton toward a hidden patch behind a buttress for the great hall, the beast gently glided to the exact spot and alighted, folding its wings away. Matt and Solon slipped silently from its back. Pressing his hand to the peryton's neck in thanks, Matt felt warmth and comfort, but something else: a feeling of disquiet. Not quite danger, but dread.

The darkness was oppressive, and the noises from the forest and the sea already had Matt's nerves on edge. He thought he'd grown to tolerate the stink of the Middle Ages, but he was wrong. He pulled the front of his hoodie up over his mouth and tried not to gag.

The entire area was thick with mud, manure, and human waste from the outhouses that had taken the brunt of the wave when it collapsed, the water washing anything not tacked down through the collapsed part of the outer wall and into the central courtyard. Hundreds of splintered pieces of wood from barrels, crockery, scythes and other field tools, stools, and benches littered the courtyard. A bloated goat's carcass floated against Matt's foot. Solon didn't seem to notice any of it.

"We need to hurry," said Matt, seeing how a stone hellhound carved into the top of the wall across the courtyard had started to twitch. Was it watching for them? "My dad will sense I'm here."

Tucked close to the wall, the boys ran toward the abbot's tower.

The monastery had been built as a fortress as much as a place of peace and learning. A high wall surrounded the main buildings with a walkway running all the way around its perimeter. Two towers flanked its corners facing the sea and the smaller island, where the newest tower stood finished, its scaffolding empty of the frenzied activity they had witnessed earlier. Like all the main buildings, the chapel built at the center of the east wall and opposite the great hall was closed up.

At the corner of the west and south walls, Solon stopped without any notice. Matt ran into his back, opening the cut above his eye on Solon's shoulder. He cursed. "Why did you stop?"

Solon pointed to a long dark shape rising and falling along the wall ahead of them. Mopping the fresh blood from his forehead, Matt slipped the penlight from his pocket, cupping his hand around the beam. He lifted the light toward the dark bulk blocking their progress.

Lined up in a row like the dead after a battle were the monks of the monastery, their cloaks covering their faces. Taking the penlight from Matt, Solon ran along the line, checking under the hoods of his sleeping comrades for Brother Renard. There was no sign of the old monk.

Solon lifted a dagger and sheath from a sleeping monk's belt and handed it to Matt to use. They were almost at the opposite corner and close to the abbot's tower when Solon lifted his hand.

Matt stopped. "What now?"

"Listen!"

Matt heard a weighty wooden whirring, like the cogs in a big mechanical clock. "What *is* that?"

"It's coming from the catacombs," whispered Solon.

Matt spotted an iron grate set at the bottom of the wall and leaned closer. The noise sounded louder and more regular, and Matt distinguished a whirring noise accompanying the mechanical sounds. The whirring reminded Matt of the gears releasing in a windup toy. Then he heard voices. Angry ones. Getting closer.

He made a decision.

"You go to the abbot's tower," he whispered, nudging Solon forward. "I'm going to find Jeannie and Brother Renard."

Solon looked shocked. "But we agreed we'd stay together!"

The foreboding Matt had felt emanating from the peryton was pressing heavily on his own chest now. It had something to do with the strange noises coming from the catacombs.

"*You* agreed," he said. "I just didn't want to argue with you."

Solon grabbed Matt's arm as he bent to lift the grate down

to the catacombs. "Don't be foolish. It is a treacherous labyrinth down there. Smugglers' tunnels stretch for miles under the bay, cutting into the catacombs of the monastery. You will never find your way alone."

The hellhound in relief in the wall above the boys stretched its neck and coughed fire into the night. Matt pulled Solon farther into the shadows.

Solon was right, he knew. As much as he wanted to find Jeannie, it wouldn't help anyone if he ended up lost in the catacombs. The hellhounds were getting agitated. Soon his dad would know they were wandering in the courtyard.

"What do you need me to do?" he asked reluctantly.

"We need to find the book first. I know what to look for, and where. While I search, you can find out if my master is locked in his room." Solon pointed to a shuttered window at the far end of the monastery. "That is his cell. Tell him I will return for him later."

"Wait," said Matt.

Sorry, Mum, he thought. He still didn't know for sure if his mum or Em was alive. He choked back his sadness. Tearing a piece of lining from his jacket, he began to draw on the tattered fabric. There was a blinding flash of white light as the animation sprang into life.

"Call me on this if you need me," Matt said, blinking to clear the dancing particles of light from his eyes and handing one of two animated walkie-talkies to Solon. "Just hold down this button here. When you finish speaking, say 'over' so I know that I can reply."

"Truly you have marvelous things in your time," Solon said, studying his walkie-talkie in fascination before clipping it onto his belt beside his bronze dagger.

THIRTY-FOUR

Em trailed a few steps behind Zach in awkward silence. With more nervous energy than she could contain, she jumped from shadow to shadow, counting them in her head, afraid she'd think or say something that would upset Zach more. She couldn't understand why he was angry with her.

Didn't boys like to kiss?

From now on, Em decided, she'd stick to imaginary snogging with boys in her books.

The closer they got to the gate, the more visible the protective shield on the wall became. It ran along the entire perimeter of the compound wall, emerging in front of Zach and Em when they took the last turn in the driveway.

Em stopped a few meters from the gate in wonder. "Wow!"

Thick vines of ivy draped over the wall like parade bunting, the tips of each leaf shimmering in a rainbow of greens. At regular intervals along the wall, the ivy hung so low it touched the ground. Thick green tendrils created a ropy chain threading through the decorative curls and knots of the massive iron gates.

"Anyone trying to get in here will need a sword to hack through those vines," signed Em, swooning dramatically in front of Zach. "Like in *Sleeping Beauty?*"

"I got it," Zach replied coldly.

Em walked over to the wall. "I've never seen so many shades of green before."

Reaching up, she touched a cluster of leaves the color of a Granny Smith apple. Expecting the leaves to be nothing more than an animation of light and color, Em was shocked when the needlepoint of a leaf pricked her finger.

"Ow!"

She jumped back as a teardrop of blood splashed onto the leaf and settled like a dot of red paint.

Are you okay, Em?

As Zach bent over Em's hand in concern, the blood spread toward the edges of the leaf, becoming part of the animation. It stretched and spread across to the next leaf, and the next one after that, on and on until there were no more leaves left within its reach, stretching deep scarlet fingers toward the sky like a plant stalk seeking the sun.

The animation was no longer a vine of ivy. Instead it was a

bloodred silhouette of a princess warrior with her broadsword extended in front of her. The protective shield had taken on the form of the last thing Em had drawn.

Zach punched the code to open the iron gates into the keypad on a small steel casing tucked under the hedge. He hit the last number just as Em caught sight of what was happening. As she gaped at the transforming clumps of ivy above their heads, she grasped a crucial problem.

The shield hadn't de-animated.

She darted between Zach and the wall.

Zach, stop!

But it was too late.

The bloody warrior princess sheathed her sword, lifted her bow, and took aim. The air filled with an impossible number of scarlet arrows, their tips shaped like ivy leaves and their fletches like roots, as if formed directly from the earth.

Em screamed and dived into the hedge as the arrows rained down. Several arrows hit her back, but instead of feeling pain, she experienced only a flash of light behind her eyes as they exploded on her skin in puffs of dust. Not one broke the skin on her arms or her legs. In the safety of the hedge, she gazed thoughtfully at the broken skin on her finger.

Zach was almost all the way under the hedgerow when an arrow tore through the hedge and drove into his calf. He yelled in pain, clutching his wounded leg, and tucked himself deeper into the bushes.

Em suddenly began to crawl out of the hedge again, back into the line of fire. Zach grabbed her.

What are you doing? Get back in here!

Pushing him off, Em crawled on, all the way out of the safe cover of the hedge, and got to her feet. She closed her eyes, raised her arms, and let the arrows swarm down on her.

THIRTY-FIVE

The first wave hit Em in a blast of scarlet and exploded against her in robust pops of red light. The second swiftly followed. Wrapped in a red fog, Em's skin felt oddly chilled, as if she had jumped into the sea in winter. Although she felt no pain, her knees started to resemble toffee as the number of arrows mounted: thirty, forty, fifty. She wanted desperately to lie down. She could no longer see the wall through the cloud of red that surrounded her. When she turned to look for Zach, it was like looking down the lens of a kaleidoscope, the scene in front of her fragmenting in slivers of color. She thought she saw him on his phone, but everything was becoming so red and she was so tired.

She collapsed to her knees. Her eyelids felt like tiny fingers were holding them closed. She shivered, then giggled for no reason. Forcing her eyes open, she lifted her hand to Zach's terri-fied face. An arrow shot into her palm and disappeared, leaving a tiny print of light on her skin before fading to nothing.

And then as quickly as it had started, the barrage stopped.

Her eyes fluttered shut.

Everything was dark.

Can you hear me, Em? Em!

Panicking, Zach shifted Em's head and shoulders onto his lap.

Why did you do that, Em? I would have been okay!

He gently brushed her forehead, releasing a puff of red dust into the air. It smelled of lavender and fresh air, of soap and . . . and sadness. It smelled of Em.

Through the gravel Zach could feel the vibrations of a vehicle coming down the lane. The Land Rover skidded to a stop a few feet away, and Simon flew out of the car toward them.

"Will she be okay?" Zach's hands were trembling so violently he could hardly form the words.

"We need to get her back inside the abbey," Simon answered, his fingers a blur. "I de-animated the shield as soon as you left the house, and had no idea it hadn't switched off before you called. Then Vaughn found this, jammed in the shield on the southwest corner of the compound."

He handed Zach a large medallion. It was identical to coins Renard had showed them up at the house but for two crucial dif-ferences. One side showed a black peryton instead of a white one.

The other showed an inverted silver spiral. "He says it's identical to the one that Malcolm stole from the cottage of a dead Animare years ago. Renard believes there were only a handful of them forged in the nineteenth century."

"It was enough to disrupt the stream without disconnecting it completely," Simon signed.

Zach dropped his eyes back to the coin. "I don't understand. Who put it there?"

"Renard sensed it belongs to Henrietta de Court," Simon signed grimly. "Her emotions were so focused when she planted it, he felt their residue on the coin. She's somewhere on the islands. And she has help."

Zach felt Em's pulse strong and steady beneath his fingers.

"I think she's asleep, son. We forget how much creative energy it takes for an Animare to animate." Simon gazed thoughtfully up at the warrior princess, bloodred and quiet, her arrows back in her quiver.

"Can we move her?" Zach signed.

Simon looked more carefully at Em's arms and legs. "She doesn't seem to have any injuries, so I don't see why not. She'd certainly be more comfortable in her bed than on this gravel."

Zach still felt confused and frightened. "But how is it possible she has no injuries? At least a hundred arrows must have hit her body."

Simon looked again at the warrior princess above them. "Em touched the shield, yes?"

"She cut her hand on one of the leaves."

Simon nodded. "Yes, blood would do it. By touching the shield in that way, Em changed it. It must've absorbed something from her extraordinary imagination." He paused and smiled at Zach. "I've a feeling that in time, we're going to witness a lot more of the impossible from Matt and Em."

Dimly, Em could sense Simon kneeling on her left, and that she was cradled in Zach's lap. She felt safer than she had in months. But the longer she stayed in this place between consciousness and unconsciousness, the more Zach's anxiety and fear were infiltrating her senses, creeping slowly and deliberately up her spine.

Oh, Em! Why did you save me?

Em's eyes opened. She smiled up at Zach.

Because I knew I could.

The air cleared of the lingering red fog, and the sun came out as Simon and Zach helped Em into the back of the Land Rover. Simon was about to start the Land Rover and turn the vehicle around when Em strained against her seat belt.

"Simon, stop!" she croaked. "We never checked to see if Grandpa's folder was on the mailbox."

Zach jumped out of the Land Rover and punched in the code again, unlocking the gates. He was gone for several minutes. When he returned, with a shake of his head and empty hands, Em noticed he was limping. A red, gooey gash gleamed on his leg, shining as if illuminated beneath the skin.

Minutes later, as they pulled up in front of the abbey, the only evidence that Zach's injury had ever existed was a smudged red tattoo on his calf. It was the size of a penny and the heart shape of an ivy leaf.

THIRTY-SIX

S olon lifted the key from under his tunic, unlocked the arched
wooden door of the abbot's tower, and slipped up the stone
steps. He had no idea what might be waiting for him at the top.

How many times had he skipped up these stairs for lessons?
He had learned what it meant to be a member of the Order of Era
Mina from his master, Brother Renard, but from the abbot he had
learned how best to prepare a skin so that it absorbed the monks'
illuminating inks slowly and evenly; how to fight with a knife and
a sword; and perhaps the best gift of all: how to read.

A strange stench filled the spiral staircase. It reminded Solon
of cabbage water that his mother would save in clay pots on the
shelf above the hearth, for use whenever any of the children were
gripped with illness. Nothing was moving. Not even a breeze from

the sea penetrated the arrow slits in the walls. Everything was eerily still.

The first door Solon reached after two flights of stairs was the abbot's bedroom. He nudged the door with his toes and it swung open. The canopied bed was empty, but someone had slept in it recently: the heavy brocade quilt was bundled at the foot of the bed and the pillows were on the floor. Monks were nothing if not fastidious, and the abbot was no exception. He would not have left his bed unmade.

Out of respect, Solon shook out the quilt and spread it neatly across the bed. When he picked up the pillows and tossed them on top of the quilts, each filled the air with a red chalky cloud.

Click-clack. Click-clack.

Something was climbing up the tower steps. Solon ducked behind the door. Slipping his bronze dagger from its sheath, he wiped his palms on his tunic and prepared to lunge.

When a black cockerel lurched into the room on scrabbling claws, Solon almost laughed with relief. Sheathing his dagger again, he climbed up the last flight of stairs to the abbot's study.

This room had been torn apart, the furnishings smashed to pieces. The abbot's chair and desk were upside down in one corner. The tapestry that the abbot had spent years supervising was in shreds on the floor.

Solon swallowed his pain. He could not do anything about the broken furniture but he could at least restore the desk and chair to their rightful positions, like he had with the abbot's bed.

As he pulled the desk back onto its feet, he noticed a piece of parchment peeking out from underneath a splintered panel of wood. Solon carefully freed the abbot's ledger, its parchment pages filled with elegant columns and figures. The abbot had clearly been working on the monastery's accounts when Matt's father had taken control of the abbey.

Solon sank into the abbot's chair, holding the ledger to his chest. He couldn't carry it with him while he and Matt searched the rest of the monastery, but it was too valuable to leave here. He needed to find a safe hiding place.

Outside he heard the hoot of an owl and the strange mechanical drone that he and Matt had heard echoing beneath the catacombs. Time was running out.

As a young novice in the monastery, the abbot had been a carpenter. Solon got to his feet again and scanned the room for some kind of secret compartment. He walked carefully around the room three times, tapping, stomping, and listening for hollows in the floor. The walls were rock solid. There was nothing.

Solon returned thoughtfully to the abbot's chair. It had been the abbot's prize and glory, carved when he himself had been an apprentice to the abbot before him.

Examining the detail in its carvings—the story of the twin perytons etched into the wood on the high back panel—Solon first tried to manipulate the arms of the chair. When nothing happened, he set it on its side and played with the legs instead, tapping and twisting them. Then he noticed something puzzling.

Viewed from underneath, the back of the chair was thicker than it looked when the chair was upright.

It took only seconds for Solon to discover that pressing and then turning the image of the white peryton on the tall back panel released a series of tiny gears. The gears whirred, clicked—and slid open.

Solon felt such a rush of adrenaline that it set him back on his heels. A manuscript wrapped in leather lay securely tucked into the secret cavity.

He lifted the manuscript out. As he did so he was hit with a roar of sound so loud that he bit his tongue. Scrambling backward in pain and shock, he dropped the folio onto the abbot's desk.

My master dedicated his life to finishing this, he thought, gazing at the leather-bound manuscript with troubled eyes. *But now he is too frail for the task.*

Carefully untying the leather straps, he opened the book.

The last beast that old Brother Renard had illuminated was the griffin, a creature with the head of a giant eagle and the body of ten lions. According to the text, the griffin was a ferocious guardian who could gallop on the ground faster than any other beast of the land. Its speed in the air was second only to the peryton.

Solon closed the book and fastened the leather straps again. After a moment's thought, he decided to return it to its little chamber. It was clear that no one else had discovered the chair's secret. It would be safe there a while longer.

Next, Solon did his best to re-create the chaos he had found when he'd entered the study. He turned over the chair and the desk again. He cleared his mind as far as he could of any thoughts of the abbot, the griffin, and, most of all, *The Book of Beasts*.

Then he left the room. He needed to catch up with Matt.

THIRTY-SEVEN

There it was again. The same whirring mechanical sound Solon and Matt had noticed before. It sounded like the shuttle of a loom shooting back and forth, and it was coming from deep in the catacombs. Solon moved across the courtyard, ears pricked, scanning the wave-shattered space for Matt.

A muffled scream echoed from the nearby woods. Solon froze. The treetops rustled. He decided it was an owl catching prey.

A lantern bobbing on a rowboat out on the water caught his attention. Darting along the broken wall of the monastery kitchens, Solon ducked for cover behind what remained of the hearth, and watched.

Two figures dragged their boat up onto the sand and tethered it to an outcropping of rocks. Solon recognized them as the gravediggers who had come to Auchinmurn to bury the dead after the Viking attack, and then remained to drink the wine from the monastery cellars. They were simpleminded, shiftless men. Solon thought it likely that Matt's father had them under his control.

"Ach," one complained, "that auld witch bit me when ah tried to feed her. Nothing more comin' tae her till dawn. And if she doesn't want it then, it'll be all the more fer me."

"Burn 'em all. That's what I say. An' ah'll keep saying it. Abomininshawns." Solon heard a gurgling sound as the second man washed his words down with a swig from a jug hooked on his fingers. "An' the de'il himself can go with the banshee for all ah care."

"Wheesht!" hissed the first. "The de'il himself will hear ye!"

Passing the jug between them in silence, the men headed unsteadily for the keep, a secure square building on the other side of the chapel where the monks kept their stores of rye, barley, and beer. At the keep's small arched doorway, Solon watched them come to a stumbling halt.

Looking around to be sure they hadn't been followed, the heavier one lifted a master key from around his neck to unlock the door. "Fancy a wee nightcap, ma friend?" he offered, waving the key under his companion's nose.

"Don't mind if ah do, noble sir."

The lock creaked and they disappeared inside.

Solon had no doubt who the "witch" was. Jeannie, the old

woman from the future who had controlled the wave. The woman Matt was so intent on finding.

He unhooked the walkie-talkie from his strap and held his finger on the button the way Matt had shown him.

THIRTY-EIGHT

Breathless and red-faced, Matt appeared at Solon's side within moments. The young scribe was gazing around in consternation, looking for the source of the rapid high-pitched squeal coming from the walkie-talkie in his hand.

"You can take your finger off the button now," Matt said.

Solon did. To everyone's relief, the squealing stopped.

"I think I know where your Jeannie is being held," Solon said.

Matt tensed. "Where?"

"In the tower on Era Mina. I saw the two drunken fools who have been taking food to her."

Matt climbed over the rubble and out onto the rocks that lined the shore. Even with the help of the opera glasses, all he could see was the faint outline of the pencil tower in the pale light of the moon. It was still amazing to him how dark it was in the Middle Ages.

"We need to get across there and see," he said, lowering the binoculars.

"Did you find my master?" Solon asked.

Matt shook his head. "The cell is empty. What happened in there? The whole room smells of bird droppings."

"One of my master's inadvertent animations." Solon untethered the gravediggers' rowboat and dragged it to the water's edge. "If your father has locked your Jeannie up in that tower, then he may have done the same to my master." He climbed in the boat and took the oars in his hands. "Are you coming?"

As Solon rowed them both toward the small island, Matt thought about animating an outboard motor. But an engine noise, of any size, in this time would call attention to them. So far they had managed to avoid his dad's notice. No point in pushing their luck, just to save a little time.

The island loomed up in front of them. The boys climbed out into the freezing, knee-deep surf, dragged the boat to a level above the tidemark, and ran to the tower.

The first thing Matt noticed was the way the door was almost two meters from the ground. Perhaps it had been built that way to avoid the tower flooding during high tides. The second was a thin, pulsing glow of an animation shield around the door's perimeter, much like the one Simon had created for the abbey. But it was the third thing that lifted his heart. He could hear singing. Melodic and merry and unmistakably Jeannie.

"Your Jeannie carries a fine tune," said Solon, looking up at the arrow slits, the only openings in the tower other than the door.

Removing his parka, Matt tore out another piece of the lining to use as a canvas, leaned against the stone wall, and began to draw. Seconds later he shoved Solon out of the way as the air above him rustled and a wooden ladder dropped from nowhere onto the sand.

After Matt had helped Solon up from the rocks, the boys maneuvered the ladder against the wall, driving its wooden legs securely into the sand.

"I'll climb," said Matt. "You watch for any changes in the door animation or for anyone coming across the bay. If I can see into the arrow slit at the top, I might be able to talk to Jeannie before we risk breaking in."

Against the backdrop of Jeannie's lilting song and the slap of the water on the rocky shore, Matt began to climb the ladder. He felt a little like a prince about to rescue Rapunzel.

THIRTY-NINE

The turret room looked like a tableau from Madame Tussauds Chamber of Horrors.

Jeannie was sitting on a bale of hay against one wall, her wrists and ankles in iron cuffs that were soldered to rings and mortared into the stones behind her. But the worst thing was the great iron mask encasing Jeannie's head, with only a narrow letter-box opening for her eyes. The mask was cuffed around Jeannie's neck and, like her wrists and ankles, soldered onto a heavy ring in the wall behind her. The air in the room was fetid and thick with dust, and lit with one stinking tallow candle.

Jeannie stopped singing the moment she saw Matt at the arrow slit.

"Mattie, I'm okay. Don't fret, son," she said in a hoarse whisper.

Her love fluttered through the crevices in the stone tower and brushed Matt's skin like a warm breeze. "And so is yer mum and Em. They got home fine."

Relief washed over him, but then such sadness that he could barely find his voice. He bit hard at the inside of his cheeks, determined not to cry. "I'll get you free, Jeannie," he said. "I promise. I have help."

Jeannie stirred. "No, son, you won't risk your life to save mine. What's about tae happen, I set in motion the moment I came back to these early days and called up that wave from beneath the islands. I upset the balance of things, and I roused Albion.

"The hollow in the earth far beneath the islands is a sacred enchanted place, a place out of time. The most powerful among our kind—those of us born on the islands and *of* the islands—are connected to this place in unique ways. Albion was the first among us, and he dwells now and forever with the beasts in Hollow Earth. During dangerous times, his descendants can communicate with him." She began coughing with a wretched, racking sound.

Solon rattled the ladder beneath Matt's feet. "Torches coming across the bay," he said. "Hurry. We need to flee this place."

Matt gripped the ladder more tightly. He couldn't leave Jeannie like this.

"But, Jeannie, if you're such a powerful Animare, can't you imagine a way out?" he asked in desperation.

"I've tried, son, but I think Malcolm has been poisoning me. I've stopped taking his food and water, but for the moment I can't imagine anything fer tuppence and my hands are useless." She rattled the iron rings on her wrists and fingers.

Poison? Matt struggled to stay focused, to keep the terror at bay. "How is my dad *doing* all of this? He's a Guardian. He can't animate anything. He's been bound in a picture for over ten years, for frick's sake!"

Jeannie's body was racked again with another coughing fit. For a second the clouds shifted, and the little cell was illuminated by a shaft of moonlight piercing the arrow slit above Matt's head. Upended on the hay next to Jeannie was a bowl and tankard. The hay under the tankard had turned purple.

"Matt, you must come down," yelled Solon. "Our enemy is almost upon us."

"I won't accept that we're helpless against him," shouted Matt through the arrow slit. "There has to be some way to stop him. If we don't, he'll find the book and use the bone quill. Then he'll control the beasts in Hollow Earth. It'll change the future. It'll change everything!"

"I know, son. I know." Jeannie's words were slurring a little. "There is only one way you might stop him."

"Tell me, Jeannie! Please!"

Jeannie tried to turn her head, but it was impossible. "Trap the grendel," she said. "Lead it into Hollow Earth. Finish *The Book of Beasts*. Complete the mission of the monks of Era Mina."

Matt thought he was going to be sick. "Jeannie, I can't . . . I don't know how to do that."

"When the time is right, son, you'll know . . . you'll know what you must do. Albion will help you. He'll get you home."

Matt could hear oars now, splashing across the water toward the tower.

"I want ye tae ken that I hoped when you and Em finally came home tae us, that we'd have much more time together," Jeannie whispered. "I'm awful sorry, son."

Matt shoved his hand through the arrow slit, desperate to reach Jeannie even though he knew it wasn't possible.

"Matt!" Solon hissed. "There's no more time!"

"I've got to go," Matt choked. "I have to go now. I'll be back for you."

Jeannie's head was drooping. The weight of the mask was too great for her to hold up for much longer. Her eyes seemed to grow smaller through the slit. Matt knew that behind the iron mask, she was smiling good-bye.

"Be brave, son. And always know that I love you and Em like my own."

Tears streaming down his cheeks, Matt climbed back to the beach.

FORTY

We may need your galaxy weapon again," said Solon, pointing at the sea as Matt climbed down the ladder.

Row upon row of Malcolm's black knights were rising up out of the waves and heading toward them, the helix symbols on their breastplates shining with a brilliant white light.

"No time, Solon, and nothing left to draw on," said Matt. He wiped his eyes, unsheathing the dagger Solon had taken from one of the sleeping monks and given to him. "We'll have to fight."

"I can draw in the sand," Solon said suddenly.

He dashed around to the other side of the tower, where he remained for several long moments. Matt had just reached the bottom of the ladder as Solon skidded back, sending a spray of sand into the air. His pride was obvious in his wide grin.

"I don't know how long my animation will work," he said. "I suggest we leave the island immediately."

"What did you do?"

Solon grinned more broadly. "I stopped the sea."

Matt stared. Malcolm's black knights continued to rise out of the water, but the first row of knights was stuck in thick swamp mud and unable to move. This had a domino effect on each successive row, forcing them to crash into the one in front, exploding each row on contact, their toxic bodies dissolving into the sea.

"Clever," said Matt, holding his fist up to bump Solon's.

Solon looked shocked. "You want to hit me now?"

"Sorry, I keep forgetting you're not Zach," Matt said, sheepishly lowering his hand. "Or Em."

Solon looked even more mystified. "You hit your family and friends?"

"Don't worry about it," said Matt, clapping the young monk on the back instead.

He was about to climb into the boat when he paused and gazed at the floundering knights out in the water.

"My dad must be watching us," he said awkwardly. "I think using the boat again is a bad idea. We'll be pretty vulnerable out there."

Solon closed his eyes. Like a stealth drone, the peryton landed next to the boys in a squall of air and sand. Matt had never been so glad to see it.

From high above the islands on the peryton's wide white back, it was possible to see the pale glow of the rising sun over the Scottish countryside.

"We don't have much time before dawn to find your master," said Matt over the beat of the peryton's wings. "Man," he added, rubbing his rumbling stomach, "I need porridge or a big slice of bread slathered with Jeannie's jam." The thought of food, and of Jeannie trapped in that hideous mask, made his stomach pitch. He blinked the tears away before Solon could see.

Solon pointed at a curl of white smoke from the hamlet outside the monastery's walls. "Someone has returned," he said. "They will have food."

The peryton swooped into a steep dive, landing with the boys at the rear of a cluster of wooden buildings surrounding a field that was divided up into quarters, each growing a different crop. Two mangy goats were tethered to a nearby fence pole, a milking bucket tipped over beneath them. Matt could hear the low mooing of a cow, but he couldn't see the animal anywhere in the cluster of buildings. The air reeked of peat, pig fat, rotting vegetables, and human waste.

"You will get used to our odors," Solon said, amused as Matt gagged at the stench. "The privy is to blame." He pointed to a hole surrounded by straw and sacks of sand. "The muck is spread over the fields before planting in the spring."

To their right stood a long rectangular thatched structure with double wooden doors open at one end and a smaller arched door at the other. A mill wheel turned in the water of the nearby stream.

Matt smelled something pleasant wafting through the open doors: bacon and wood smoke. His stomach betrayed him once again.

"This is James Guthrie's cottage," said Solon, starting forward. "The miller. He lives here with his children, Fraser the gatekeeper and his daughter. Perhaps he will give us some food."

The main room in the miller's cottage was warm and dark, the shutters on the windows closed against the chill of the morning. It was comfortably furnished with wooden chairs covered with sheepskin; deer pelts covered the walls for insulation, and an open sleeping loft stretching the length of the structure was lined with straw. A sturdy table carved from pine was laid for a meal, and warm bread was set on a warming stone in an open hearth in the center of the long room. A pig was rotating on a spit above smoldering slabs of peat; a cauldron of turnips simmered gently on the fire. But the cottage's inhabitants were nowhere to be seen.

Matt stepped closer to the sizzling meat and inhaled. Carik's fat rabbit felt like hours ago.

"We have got to have some of this," he said.

But Solon had moved past the hearth. Matt followed him, looking wistfully over his shoulder at the roasting meat.

At the farthest end of the room was a fenced pen, behind which stood the cow Matt had heard mooing earlier. He stopped in amazement, gazing at the cow and a litter of squealing wild pigs at its feet.

"The animals live in the same room as the people?" he said in disgust.

"Of course." Solon was gazing around the cottage with a frown on his face. "That cow and those pigs are more important to this family than some of their relatives."

Matt experienced an unsettling rush of emotion coming from his companion. "What's wrong?" he asked. "You're worried."

Solon lifted the gate to the animal's pen and went inside.

The straw is fresh and the animals have recently been fed," he said, coming out again. "So where are James and his bairns? And the others that live here—Fraser the monastery gatekeeper and his daughter, Jo? My sister Margaret oftentimes cooks for them. They would never leave the hearth untended like this. This emptiness disturbs me."

Hunger was overwhelming Matt's senses. It had been days since he'd eaten anything substantial. "I can't think about anything else until I've eaten," he blurted.

He unsheathed the knife Solon had given him, wiped it on his jeans, and cut a thick slice of meat from the thickest part of the pig. Then he sat at the table, tore a chunk from the warm bread, wrapped it around the meat, and crammed it into his mouth. The crispy skin on the pork burned the roof of his mouth, but it was worth it.

"To roast a pig is a long process," Solon said, still looking around. "It's early in the day still. This is all very mystifying."

A tall robed figure appeared out of the shadows of the animal pen.

"Then allow me to explain," it drawled.

FORTY-ONE

Em knew she was being followed the moment she stepped off the garden path and turned into the rows of raspberry bushes that bordered Jeannie's kitchen garden. The night was clear and the moon bright, but like most evenings in this part of Scotland it was chilly and damp and every plant in the garden was heavy with moisture. At first Em thought she was feeling the heaviness of the humidity on her skin, but after a few more steps beyond the garden she was convinced she felt a presence nearby.

She'd sneaked out of bed and outside as soon as the abbey had quieted, her body none the worse for the animated arrow wounds. Having listened outside Zach's door until she no longer heard movement, she had then crept down the back stairs and out through a door she'd drawn and animated at the back of the pantry.

Two more steps and she felt it again. Closer this time. A prickling on her skin, a kind of internal goose bumps. She quickened her pace through the bushes and cut back in toward the garden, ignoring the occasional scratch from the branches and pulling up the hood of Matt's sweatshirt, which she'd been wearing for days. She could smell him in the fabric, and refused to let her mum wash it.

Were those footsteps?

Em glanced around. Jeannie's garden was bordered with fruit trees in full bloom, but in the quarter acre of tilled space, other than the prickly berry bushes behind which she now crouched, there were not a lot of places to hide—even in the dark.

Whatever it was, was moving closer. She had to find a hiding place, and fast. Quickly pulling her sketch pad from her pocket, she sat cross-legged in the darkness and began to draw.

A trellis sprouted from the ground, complete with thick vines and roses growing through the latticework. Each rose had a tiny twinkle of light at its center that looked ethereal, magical. The heavy scent of roses fought for Em's attention with Jeannie's lavender and sweet basil as she ducked behind the verdant tangle.

She heard the telltale click of the garden gate and shivered, clutching tightly to the only item approaching a weapon that she had, preparing herself for something horrible to emerge from the shadows up ahead.

Wisps of clouds floated past the moon. A gull screeched over the bay.

A hand grabbed Em's shoulder.

Em pivoted and charged, knocking Zach into a patch of rhubarb. *Get off me, Em!*

Em's heart was hammering so hard she could barely hear herself think, let alone Zach as well. *Jeez, I could have really hurt you, you idiot! What are you doing sneaking around in the dark?*

Oh, funny you should ask. Zach stood up, pulling leaves from his hair. *And you couldn't have hurt me with your sketch pad.*

Em held up a pair of pinking shears and glared. *I could have done some serious damage with these, though.*

Zach glared back, his thoughts flying fast and angry into Em's head. *What are you doing out here? You know we shouldn't leave the abbey after dark.*

I was taking a walk.

With pinking shears and a sketch pad?

Zach put his hands on Em's shoulders. She felt the full force of his determination. *The truth this time. You've obviously been taking this little walk for the last few nights.*

How do you know?

Too much muck on your wellies and it's only been wet at night.

Em pulled away from him sulkily. *You think you're so smart, Sherlock!*

Picking up her sketch pad from under the rhubarb where it had landed, she waved Zach forward, resigned.

If I show you something, it has to be our secret.

Don't you think your family has enough secrets to last a lifetime?

"Funny," Em signed, punctuating her response with an extra gesture. *I mean it, Zach. I need your word.*

Fine. In the meantime, what happens to that?

He nodded at the animated trellis.

Ripping out the page, Em shredded her drawing. The trellis blazed brightly for a few seconds, then, as if someone were snuffing out candles, each twinkling bloom puffed out one at a time. Finally, the trellis sank into the ground and disappeared.

Keeping to the shadows, Em led Zach toward Jeannie's potting shed.

Two silhouettes standing at Sandie's sitting-room window watched the telltale light of Em's trellis animation fade to nothingness.

"What's she up to?" Vaughn asked.

"I wish I knew," Sandie said, watching. "Simon and Renard have taught her well. She's keeping a lot locked in her mind at the moment."

Outside the window an owl hooted. Sandie saw it glide out of a nearby pine tree, swoop to the ground, and rise into the night sky with a wriggling rabbit gripped in its claws. She felt like that rabbit: battered, torn, and heading toward the end. Turning away from the window, she took Vaughn's hand and led him from the room.

Out in the darkness, a thin line of light glowed around the potting-shed door.

FORTY-TWO

As they stopped at the door to the potting shed, Zach looked at Em.

"If I know you've been sneaking out, your mum likely does too," he signed.

"She's afraid I'll snap under the strain." Em lowered her hands. Telepathy was easier in the darkness. *But I won't. I'm stronger than that.*

She pulled the key for the shed from her pocket and unlocked the door. Before she opened it enough for them to slip inside, she put her hand on Zach's chest.

I need you to swear on your powers as a Guardian that this will be our secret. Otherwise, no way you're seeing what's in here.

With her purple-streaked hair, her pale skin, and her fierce determination, in that moment Em looked years older than thirteen. Zach nodded.

I swear.

Inside, the shed smelled of manure, motor oil, and cut grass. The ride-on mower was parked to one side, and behind it stood a wall of rickety wooden shelves loaded with clay flowerpots, bags of seeds, and a sundry assortment of gardening tools. Pitchforks, spades, and two rakes stood in the corner.

On the other side of the shed was a worn armchair and a stack of books. A small window covered in dirt and cobwebs was in the middle of the back wall, the hazy moon visible above the silhouette of Era Mina.

You're in here secretly reading?

Zach was about to walk farther into the shed when Em grabbed his arm.

Stop! There are things I need to switch off.

Zach watched as Em followed the extension cord plugged in behind a large clay pot and running along behind sacks of mulch, leading up to a projector and Em's iPad on a shelf.

You're throwing a hologram against the wall? Zach glanced around, clearly trying to work out which items in the shed weren't real. *Why not just animate something?*

Em rolled her eyes. *Because everyone in the abbey who might follow me would recognize an animation immediately.*

Lifting down the iPad, she closed the program. One by one, the comfy chair, the stack of books, and then the entire back wall of the shed shimmered and pixilated. Each image faded to black, leaving a makeshift green screen standing between them and the real back half of the shed.

Carefully, Em pulled down the screen. Zach laughed in amazement. Bunches of herbs, turnips, and leafy plants hung from a clothesline strung across the back of the hut, each bunch in varying degrees of dehydration, along with the dried-out carcass of a squirrel. Apart from a blue plastic tarpaulin covering a canvas the size of a flat-screen TV that was leaning against the wall, all the tableau needed was a blazing hearth, a pot of porridge, and a skinned rabbit or two hanging from the rafters to complete the picture of an old crofter's cottage in the eighteenth century.

Zach looked up at the squirrel and recoiled. "Gross!"

"I didn't kill it, in case you're wondering," Em signed back. "It was roadkill."

"Oh, good. That makes me feel much better!"

"It's not as bad as it looks." Em looked around, thinking about this from Zach's perspective. "Okay. It looks bad."

Jeannie's pestle and mortar and Simon's missing clay bowls were spread on a table next to the blue-tarped canvas, along with what looked like a chunk of the Auchinmurn hillside. Zach poked his finger into a plastic bag caked inside with a dark, sticky substance, and rubbed his fingertips together.

Is this blood?

Em nodded, holding up the palm of her left hand with a

Band-Aid on it. *I mixed the squirrel's blood with some of my own.*

Zach pulled a face. *Jeez, Em. What are you doing in here?*

Em could feel his concern heavy on her shoulders. With great care she pulled the blue tarp from the canvas underneath.

It was the missing medieval triptych from the abbey.

Em had painted over the picture of Daniel in the lion's den that had been there before. Now the whole painting leaped from the canvas at multiple points the way a 3-D movie might, an intense heat pulsing from each of the three panels.

The central panel showed a number of strange, skeletal-looking knights surrounding Era Mina's finished pencil tower, wearing armor embossed with wings on their shoulder plates and silver helixes on their breastplates. Each had only half a face. A tall, leaderlike figure stood among them, his head tilted back, his long hair painted in broad, expressionist strokes like Cézanne or Monet might have used. A rough-hewn, slobbering mud creature dominated the background.

The panel on the right showed a cave opening in the cliff, which Em had rendered in a maelstrom of grays, yellows, and blacks. The cave mouth seemed to be pursing, as if in a kiss. The left panel was unfinished.

"I think the tall one in the middle panel's my dad," Em said. She could hardly bring herself to look at the image, even now.

"It's stunning, Em," Zach signed. "The best thing you've ever painted."

"You think?"

"But what is it? Why have you painted it?"

"I have an idea and it has to do with Albion."

Zach frowned. "What are you talking about?"

FORTY-THREE

Solon drew his sword. Matt scrambled up from the table, knocking over his chair and spilling his food as Malcolm Calder walked into the light.

He swept his cloak behind his shoulders, revealing the beauty of his polished armor—the silver helix on his breastplate that appeared to pulse with the rhythm of his heart, the leather sheath hooked on to his wide belt protecting the bone quill. He slipped the hood from his head, revealing the full horror of his deformed mouth, his unfinished lips, and the shadowy, viscous holes where teeth should have been. When he spoke, his tongue flicked into those cavities, sending clouds of black powder into the air.

"You may join us now," he called softly up to the loft space.

Scared eyes blinked against the light as the inhabitants of

the house emerged from the loft. Two men, two women, and two children: a girl and a boy. James Guthrie the miller was a round man with flour on his apron. The gatekeeper Fraser was frail with stringy gray hair. Matt guessed that his daughter—Solon had said her name was Jo—was in her twenties, but he couldn't be sure. People aged faster in the Middle Ages, a result of a poor diet, poor living conditions, and no understanding of germs or diseases. If a man lived into his fifties during this century, he was lucky.

Matt felt a wave of fear emanating from Solon at the sight of the second young woman. He guessed with a lurch in his stomach that this was Margaret, Solon's sister.

Malcolm said nothing more until everyone was seated around the table, the children huddled close to their father the miller. Solon exchanged a long look with his sister. Margaret smiled in return, an expression that suggested absolute faith in her brother and his friend. Matt wished he was brimming with the same sense of confidence. He could feel Solon's entire being pulsing with hate.

"Take a seat, boys," said Malcolm. "I asked Margaret to prepare this feast for us all, and it would be a shame not to eat it."

The miller's son turned from Malcolm and buried his head in his father's shoulder. His older sister did not turn away from the abomination now sitting at the head of the table.

"Let us begin," said Malcolm.

Margaret began silently ladling mashed turnip into the bowls on the table. Malcolm looked disapprovingly at the wedge of missing flesh that Matt had taken from the roasting pig before carving the rest himself, his tongue flickering, lizardlike, between unfinished gums.

Matt sensed that Solon was plotting to attack at any moment. He switched his knife to his left hand in preparation, shoving his right into his pocket and grasping for his pencil.

"Boys," said Malcolm, licking pig fat from his fingers, "before you do anything foolish, you may want to take a wee gander out the window. Perhaps what you see will persuade you to join us for this delicious meal."

The sheer force of will surging from Malcolm felt to Matt like trying to stand upright against the wind on the ferry to Auchinmurn. He automatically turned toward the window, lifted the latch on the shutters, and pushed them open.

Outside, the hamlet was encircled with Malcolm's black knights, their breastplates blazing, their half faces expressionless.

"How is your father managing this?" whispered Solon beside Matt. "How does he keep this legion of knights animated?"

Matt had asked Jeannie a similar question. Guardians couldn't animate. All of this was *impossible*.

The dark knights stood motionless at the tree line. Matt figured if he and Solon attempted to animate, they would be attacked in a moment.

"Of course they would stop you," said Malcolm.

Matt jerked back from the window at the sound of his father's voice.

"But I wouldn't set them all on you at once," Malcolm continued. "Especially not you, Mattie. My own flesh and blood." He swallowed a piece of meat without chewing it. "Besides, I have a more important task for you in mind."

With a sudden brutal movement, Malcolm stabbed the carving knife into the table and snatched the little boy from the miller's arms.

"Watt!" Guthrie leaped from his chair and tried to grab his son.

Little Watt squirmed madly to get back to his father. Then he calmed, stopped bucking, and snuggled against Malcolm's shoulder. Guthrie ceased fighting too. He slumped back on his chair, smiling blandly at Malcolm.

Old Fraser stirred on the opposite side of the table. Margaret was at his side in a moment, one hand on the old man's shoulder and the other on his daughter Jo's, calming them. Matt sensed Margaret's desire to keep the situation under control, her willingness to comply with Malcolm's wishes. She too was a victim of his powerful mind control.

Matt didn't need his Guardian powers to work out his father's intentions. Malcolm was willing to inspirit these villagers and hurt them, to force Solon and Matt to obey.

"I'm glad that I'm making myself clear," Malcolm said, joggling Watt against his shoulder and cooing into Watt's ear. Bursts of charcoal dust erupted from the incomplete side of his face as it touched the boy's smooth, rounded cheek.

The faceless knights had shifted closer, pressed against the building. Matt slammed the shutters. Solon dropped the wooden latch.

Malcolm nodded, satisfied. "Good."

He returned Watt to his father's lap. Margaret returned to the turnips. A grim silence settled over the table.

"Sit," bellowed Malcolm suddenly, his words erupting in a cloud of chalky darkness.

Matt and Solon sat.

FORTY-FOUR

Matt had lost his appetite. He moved the food around on his plate, his mind grappling for a way out. How he and Solon might extricate themselves from Malcolm's power. How they had to free Jeannie and find Solon's master. He didn't dare dwell on these thoughts for long. His father would read them too easily.

Next to Matt, Solon was shoveling turnips and bread into his mouth. Malcolm watched the boys intently, glancing out of the open door at the fields outside every minute or two. The sun was up. Shadows moved through the treetops.

Was his father waiting for someone?

Matt attempted to pry inside his father's mind. He couldn't read any emotion there at all. No matter how hard he pressed, he could not push through the steely firewall in Malcolm Calder's head. Matt's grandfather Renard used a similar strategy when he wanted to keep Em and Matt from reading his emotions, only Renard's mind projected an old caravan sitting on sand dunes.

Matt turned to Solon. "How can you eat right now?" he hissed.

"In this world, you eat when there's food in front of you," Solon said with a shrug. "Who knows when we will see a full plate again? Besides, our Margaret knows how to roast a pig."

Margaret scooped another helping of turnips into Solon's bowl. As she walked past, she flicked Solon's ear with her fingers. Matt saw Solon look into his bowl. A string of knotted thread lay on top of the turnips. In his next spoonful, Solon tucked the thread under his tongue.

Malcolm wolfed down most of the pork. Matt forced himself to eat his turnips to quiet his rumbling stomach. He did his best not to dwell on the knotted thread. If he was trying his hardest to get into his father's mind, then certainly Malcolm was doing the same in return.

No one looked up from their plates until they were empty. Malcolm took one last glance outside and then stood.

"Boys, you will return with me to the monastery," he said. "Margaret will remain here with the others under—my protection, shall we say? When you have completed the tasks I have in mind for you, she and the others will be free to go, to leave the island and join their families on the mainland. Understood?"

"Understood," said Matt, willing Solon to remain silent lest he reveal the thread in his mouth.

They left the cottage. At the tree line bordering the hamlet, Malcolm stopped and lifted his hand in front of the good side of his face, blocking the sun. Then he spread his fingers open and stared at the sky. He repeated this odd gesture with his hands two more times.

"What's he doing?" Matt whispered to Solon.

Solon spat the little thread into his hand, concealing it in his palm. "Measuring time," he answered. "Does your world not need to do that anymore?"

"Of course," said Matt, watching his father in curiosity. "But we have clocks."

"I have heard of clocks," said Solon. "But I have not seen one."

Matt would have explained further, but he could see that Solon was fingering the knots on the thread with a look of concentration on his face.

"Are you reading that?" Matt said, watching more closely.

"My sister has left a message for me in the knots. *Keep your secrets.*"

"What does it mean?"

"The book," he said softly. "She means *The Book of Beasts.*"

Malcolm had turned back toward the hamlet and was facing Matt and Solon. He closed his eyes and began to count down from ten.

"Nine . . . eight . . . seven . . ."

A chill swept toward the hamlet from the forest. Matt's scalp tingled, his mind bombarded with fierce colors and a piercing light.

"Six . . . five . . ."

Solon yelped, sliding to the ground with his back against a tree trunk and his head in his hands.

"Two . . . one and . . . bravo!"

Matt found that he was crouched on the ground, his hands over his head. His eyes watered with floaters of white light. He stared at the place they had come from, refusing to believe what he saw.

The knights were gone. James Guthrie's cottage no longer had windows or doors or even a chimney. Its roof had been flattened, and the ground on which it stood had somehow become a swamp. The building shimmered lightly as it slowly sank into the ground, sealed like a giant coffin.

FORTY-FIVE

Matt gawked at the swamp. His father's actions had stunned him. The same question thundered in his head, clashing with his fears for those trapped inside the sinking cottage.

How could a Guardian create such a powerful animation?

"Margaret!" Solon shouted in horror. He scrambled toward the swamp, but stopped hopelessly as the roof gently sank from sight. "Margaret!"

"Touching." Malcolm shrugged. "But a waste of time. They will be safe if you do as I ask. We'll take the path through the forest to the monastery."

Matt's feet were moving against his will toward the path. Solon followed wordlessly.

They reached the perimeter of the monastery buildings in

minutes. Without pausing, Malcolm walked past the sleeping monks and straight into the chapel. Matt realized that his father was heading for the rear of the altar.

Lifting a flaming torch from a nearby holder, Malcolm held open the door to the catacombs.

"In you go," he said, and pushed the boys down the narrow, slippery stone steps in front of him. "Lead the way, Solon."

It took a few minutes to adjust to the smell of rotting vegetation and stagnant water. Matt used the nauseating odor to help him lock his thoughts away from his dad. He noticed that Solon was clenching his teeth, his jaw muscle flexing as he blocked Malcolm too.

The darkness was heavy with dampness and dread, both of which pressed down on Matt's shoulders as they slogged along tunnels flooded with water from Jeannie's wave.

They entered the burial chamber of the monastery's saints and martyrs. Several sleeping forms were lined up beside the damp walls; others lay next to sarcophagi or on top of tombs. All were asleep in deep inspirited comas, Matt was relieved to see, and breathing comfortably.

"Where is my master?" said Solon, checking beneath the cowls of his nearby sleeping comrades.

"Not here," said Malcolm, moving on through the catacombs. "I will take you to him, never fear. And then you will do something for me."

The farther they trudged, the deeper they seemed to be going.

The tunnel ceiling was so low now that Malcolm could no longer stand up straight. Matt could feel his chest tightening at the sense of claustrophobia.

"Where are you taking us?" Solon demanded as they walked on.

Matt's stomach clenched. He thought all the monks would know these tunnels. If Solon didn't know where Malcolm was taking them, then they were really lost.

FORTY-SIX

I have to go back to the beginning for you," signed Em, "or you'll never understand."

She lowered her hands and thought for a moment. Then she lifted them again. "I know this sounds crazy, but I think the ghostly presence who appeared in my room is Albion. The First Animare, the guy who guards the beasts in Hollow Earth."

Zach gazed at the swirling image of the cave in the picture. "So is that . . ."

"It's the image swirling behind the presence when it's in my room. The scene Duncan Fox painted. The picture Dad tried to make me and Matt go into when we were toddlers. The original is kept down in the abbey vaults, but I've seen copies since." Em tapped the canvas. "When Grandpa told us all that Hollow Earth exists outside time, then I figured Albion must be outside time too. For some reason he showed himself to me."

Zach flopped onto a sack of mulch as if his legs wouldn't hold him up anymore.

"How many times has Albion appeared to you?"

"Three times. The first time, he almost pulled me into Hollow Earth itself."

"Are you kidding me?" signed Zach angrily. "Why didn't you say something?"

"Don't worry; it never happened again," Em rushed on. "But I felt this desperate desire to draw. Every time he appeared, I sketched what came into my imagination."

"Albion was putting the images in your mind?"

Em nodded. "And a few nights ago I realized what I had to do with the sketches. I had to paint them, using only materials they would have used in the Middle Ages."

Zach stared at the painting. "So you've used inks made from plants and leaves?"

"Yup," said Em. "I now know so much about what you can do with lupines that I could cure gout . . . whatever that is."

She went over to the table and returned with one of Simon's prehistoric clay pots with a golden honeylike substance inside.

"Did you know that the color white was the hardest to make back then, so to capture light artists literally illuminated their art with flakes of gold?" She handed the pot to Zach, who sniffed it warily. "I had to make do with honey and crushed sunflowers."

Zach's gaze settled more closely on the image of the cave mouth. He touched the canvas with his pinkie, the paint still wet in places. Em suddenly sensed his mind exploding. As he pressed his hands to his ears, a blast of thought streamed into her head.

Screaming . . . I can feel screaming. I have never felt screaming before . . .

Em felt scared and excited. *Someone's screaming?*

Not someone, something. . . . It's going right through me. . . . Argh! The pain . . . Zach stumbled backward, knocking into Em. *Jeez, Em. It's like . . . you've painted yourself into this. Your feelings, your memories, maybe . . . I don't understand. . . . What have you done? Why have you painted this?*

Em blazed with fierce pride. It was working!

"Promise you won't think I'm crazy?" she signed.

He sat up shakily. "No guarantees. Look at this place. There's a dead squirrel hanging from the rafters."

Em took a deep breath. "I'm going to use this painting to travel back in time to rescue Matt and Jeannie."

Zach's eyes widened. Em rushed on before he tried to talk her out of it.

"Think about it! What if I can connect myself to the right time period with art that I've made with medieval materials?"

Zach stood up angrily, shaking his head. *You're not traveling back to the Middle Ages, Em. Even if this does work, you can't go back alone.*

Then come with me.

Come on, are you serious?

Em could sense Zach trying to inspirit her, calm her, and make her change her mind. But she was prepared. She had known that he'd discover her secret sooner rather than later. They were too close for him not to. As Zach tried to work on her mind, she focused on his, digging through his empathy and his love and getting to his anger at her and his frustration at Matt. She poked at it, shone a light onto it.

Stop it, Em!

You first!

They collapsed next to each other on a sack of potting soil, both holding their hands to their heads. Zach surrendered first.

"You win!" he signed irritably. "I'll come. But how do you know for sure it's going to work? And if it gets you there, how can it get us back to the present?"

"I don't know," Em admitted.

It was impossible to keep her fears to herself any longer.

Zach took her hand. *Talk to me.*

Gratefully Em let her worries wash through her, into Zach's waiting mind.

The panel on the left isn't the entire image that comes to me. But I can't . . . I can't bring myself to put on this canvas what I'm actually seeing.

You must. It might help us figure out what to do.

Em nodded, biting her lip. Zach was right.

She moved to the table and mixed some paints. Her shoulders

relaxed, and her hair fell forward, the purple streak framing her cheek like a comma as she turned to the canvas and applied the paint to the unfinished panel. She painted with a fierce concentration, but without the intention of animating. The image stayed flat and obedient on the canvas.

Em laid down her brush and pointed silently at what she had revealed.

FORTY-SEVEN

Matt had lost his bearings entirely.

They were waist deep in water now, their pace slowing considerably. At one point the water had reached as high as their chests, and they'd had to dog-paddle through it. The tunnel pressed in on them, dark and cold and growing ever smaller.

The tunnel suddenly opened up, offering a pocket that was less a chamber than a rock formation. It was enough to give the boys a chance to catch their breath.

"Almost there!" said Malcolm. He sounded almost cheerful, as if they were out hiking in the countryside, heading toward a picnic instead of a terrible unknown.

He's mad, Matt realized. Unbound after ten years inside a painting, his father had clearly lost his humanity as well as his face.

Malcolm prodded them on. His excitement was growing pal-pable. Matt quietly animated a compass on what was left of the lining in his jacket. Hiding it beneath his sleeve, he watched the needle bounce around and settle. They were tramping west.

Matt couldn't believe it. They couldn't be heading west. West was the bay. West was water. Deep water.

They'd now been gone all of the night and most of the morn-ing. He wondered if Carik was searching for them. He was beyond tired now, running on pure adrenaline spiked with fear.

The disturbing mechanical sound Matt and Solon had heard reverberating under the grounds of the monastery suddenly began echoing up ahead. Whatever was making the noise was moving toward them. The tunnel walls shook. Dirt and stones began to drop from the roof of the tunnel, raining on them.

"Pick up the pace, boys," Malcolm advised. "I don't want to have to dig you out from a cave-in."

The tunnel ended in a sheer drop to a vast internal cavern. From their position on the precipice, Matt stared into the cham-ber below. Ancient cave etchings met his eyes. A hellhound snarling in relief. The peryton, its wings so lifelike they appeared to be fluttering.

"I know where we are," he said in astonishment. "I was here in the summer. This is Solon's Cave." He stared at his white-faced companion. "It's named after you."

Solon looked terrified. "This is the place of the portal to the world of the beasts," he said. "This is where I brought the peryton into the world above, with my master's help. It's how we saved the village when the Vikings came."

"Awesome!" said Matt, for a second forgetting the danger they were in, forgetting the threat to Solon's family at the overwhelming sense of being a part of history.

He didn't forget for long. Rolling out of the darkness beneath them was an enormous mechanical monster like nothing Matt had ever seen.

At the center of the beast was trapped the body of a man.

FORTY-EIGHT

E m's picture was of Matt.

"His hair is a bit longer," Em signed, swallowing, "but I think maybe time is passing differently for him. You know?"

Matt was standing beneath a gloomy archway, leaning forward at an odd angle. He was wounded. The hilt of a small weapon stuck out from his side, right above his hip bone.

Em was pale. *That's why we need to get back there. To help him.*

Zach looked at her with concern in his eyes. *It doesn't look like a knife.*

Em shook her head. *It's the bone quill. The ancient object that you use to animate the beasts and free them from Hollow Earth.*

Matt gets stabbed by it! Are you even sure this is Matt?

"I don't know!" Em cried, forgetting to either sign or telepath in her anguish. "But I can't risk it!"

"If this did come into your imagination from Albion," Zach signed swiftly, "then we need help. Matt's hurt. We have to tell someone."

"Not yet! You promised!" Em jabbed a finger at the triptych. "I wish I knew how the panels are connected. They seem fragmented. Like I'm watching a movie that's been put together out of order."

Em had captured the pencil tower on Era Mina in loose, sketchy strokes. Along with the telltale halo of an animation inside the tower itself, there was a huge hole between two of the arrow slits at the top. It looked like a powerful projectile of some kind had hit the wall.

Zach picked up a book on medieval art from Em's jumble of papers. He flipped to the section on altar adorations and triptychs, then passed it to Em.

"It says here that the central panel of a triptych is often just the most dramatic part of the message, and the panels are not necessarily in sequential order," he signed.

Like a comic, Em telepathed, reading swiftly.

Zach nodded. *Think about how comics are laid out on the page. You read the huge central panel first. Then you go to the smaller surrounding panels to get the bigger picture. Does that help?*

Em felt a jolt of hope. *If that's the case, maybe some of this stuff hasn't happened yet. Maybe Matt's okay. Zach, I love you!*

She threw herself into Zach's arms, knocking them down together onto the sacks of potting soil lined up against the wall of the shed.

"Sorry," she signed, giggling as she got up again. "If any of this is going to work, I think I need just one more thing before I . . . we try. And I need it soon. Help me get this place straight again, will you?"

Zach worked with Em to set up the hut the way it had been when they had entered. He couldn't help himself. He wished she would kiss him again.

FORTY-NINE

Middle Ages

The clanking, whirring gears of the ghastly contraption were shaking loose stalactites from the cavern's uneven ceiling. Its frame was huge, its shape resembling a winged demon of the undead. The whole mechanism reminded Matt of a terrible torture device.

Instead of legs, the machine had a set of wooden wheels on the far edges and connected to them a series of cogs, ranging in size from that of a teacup to as big as a bicycle wheel. They turned a complex system of gears, belts, and chains, all powered by one of Malcolm's skeletal half-faced minions on a treadle, sending sparks of light and energy to the place where Brother Renard was bound. From the front, the old monk looked as if he was being carried on the back of a hideous wraith.

Before Matt could stop him, Solon had leaped from the lip of the tunnel, landing hard on his feet in the cavern below. He scrambled to his trapped master, reaching around the machine's wooden wings to loosen the thick leather straps around Brother Renard's ankles. The moment he touched the straps, an electric current sliced across the palms of his hands, throwing him back against the dirt floor. Matt leaped down to join him, stumbling on impact, feeling the shock jar his body.

"Let my master go," Solon yelled, nursing his blistered hands as Malcolm climbed down a rope ladder hooked into the rock face and strolled across the cavern toward the machine. "Use me for your schemes, for your animations. Brother Renard is old and weak-minded!"

"And that is why I have such control over him," Malcolm said. "His mind is utterly broken. With very little practice, I've been able to project images into his mind that he is then able to animate for me."

Brother Renard's head was locked in an iron mask, like the one that trapped Jeannie. His feet were strapped in leg irons, and his fingers were held in fingerless gloves of iron linked to a wooden tablet covered with a piece of parchment. Matt's stomach lurched in disgust. The old monk's fingers were covered in pinpricks, many scabbed over but several dripping onto the parchment. The old Animare had been drawing with his own blood.

Brother Renard was like a marionette, but the strings were

controlling his mind, not his limbs. Matt shivered. Is this what would become of all Animare if evil Guardians like Malcolm controlled them?

Matt's father ran his hand lovingly along the sleeping monk's arm. "Ingenious, don't you think?" he said.

"It's despicable!" Solon said.

Malcolm was ready as Solon flew at him, striking the boy across the side of his head and knocking him against the rock. "All this drama for a weak old man," he said. Matt and Solon's reaction seemed to disappoint him. He reared up taller. "My contraption is a work of genius!"

Matt dared himself to stare directly into his father's ruined face. "How did you know we would come to the miller's cottage?"

"I found an accomplice following you after you left the tower on Era Mina. . . . Unwilling, but helpful nonetheless."

He moved to the far corner of the cavern and dragged Carik from the shadows.

She was gagged, her eyes glazed and her lids puffy from sleep. Her fury lay like an orange sheen against her alabaster skin.

Solon ran to her, trying to gather her in his arms. She pushed him away, tearing the rag from her mouth, spitting and coughing phlegm into the dirt.

"What have you done to her?" Solon shouted.

"Relax, young man." The helix on Malcolm's breastplate spun and sparked with light whenever he moved closer to the cave paintings. "I encouraged her cooperation with a little mind control.

Nothing more. She will recover quickly, I am sure. She's been resting nicely since I found her."

He ruffled Carik's spiky blond hair. She slapped his hand away furiously. Malcolm laughed.

"Her mind has been quite entertaining, though." He winked at Solon. "This young Viking is quite smitten with you, my lad, even if she's angry with you for abandoning her in the cave. She blames you for that, Mattie. It seems she heard you leave, and followed you as far as the abbey, where, thankfully, I intercepted her."

Carik's fury was rising. She shifted closer to Solon, glaring at Matt.

Matt needed to think. Ideally without worrying about a furious girl getting in the way. Em was crazy enough when she was angry, but she at least didn't carry weapons. He shrugged at Carik apologetically. He didn't have any extra energy to worry about hurting her feelings.

Brother Renard stirred. Lifting the iron mask, Malcolm stared into the old monk's tired eyes.

"It won't be long now," he said soothingly. "Death will come soon enough."

Solon threw himself toward Malcolm. "The devil take you to hell!" he yelled.

Caught unawares, Malcolm stumbled against the machine. The tablet fell from the old monk's feeble fingers and bounced onto the ground.

Matt dived at the tablet before his father could reach it, and crushed it under his feet, grinding it to splinters.

"Draw that," he said.

Malcolm howled with rage, sending a burst of red dust into the air. He swung at Matt, who threw himself backward against the cave wall.

With an animal yell, Carik leaped up onto Malcolm's back, yanking viciously at his hair. He was too strong for her, knocking her from his shoulders like a bug. She landed on her back with a grunt, the wind knocked from her lungs.

"No," Malcolm screamed, whirling back to where Solon was trying to release the old monk from the machine.

Without the old Animare in his power, Matt knew that his dad would need to depend only on his Guardian powers. If Matt could draw something to help Solon, then perhaps they would stand a chance of defeating him.

He dug in his pocket for his nub of charcoal, taking his eyes and his concentration from his father.

FIFTY

A custard-colored moon was shedding its pale light on the ancient standing stones at the Devil's Dyke, high on the island of Auchinmurn. By the light of her headlamp Em worked quickly, scraping the yellow lichen from the ancient stones into a small plastic bag. If everything went to plan, this extra lichen and the stone scrapings would be the final element for her painting. She hoped the scrapings would be ancient enough, would make the triptych more authentic.

Through the gloaming Em could see the dark shape of a crofter's crumbling blackhouse. She froze in shock at the feeling of an ice-cold hand on the back of her neck.

"Tell yer story walking, lass," growled the old man. His hand slid to her hoodie and hauled her away from the stones.

"Hey," Em exclaimed, struggling in his strong grip. "You're hurting me! What do you want? What have I done?"

Her mind slid wildly through the possibilities as the old man pushed her wordlessly through the forest of tall pines and down the craggy hillside. She wasn't trespassing. As far as she knew, there was no preservation order on the stones. Why was he so angry?

Despite his age—Em judged him to be as old as her grandfather—the man was surprisingly fast. Every few steps Em had to skip a little to keep up.

It was the middle of the night and a chilling fog was seeping in from the sea, covering the ground. Em kept stubbing her toes on roots. The man's stride was long and unrelenting.

"You're one of them abbey weans, aren't ye?" he barked.

Em wriggled her shoulders, trying to slip out of her hoodie, but the straps of her backpack made freeing herself impossible. "What if I am?"

He didn't answer.

They slowed a little as they crested the hill and began to climb down toward the footpath. Em decided to try another tack, going limp and relaxing every part of her body. Instead of slowing, the man only lowered his arm, letting Em slide across the rough ground behind him. Her shins smashed against a rock.

"Ow! Now you're really hurting me!"

"Ach, stop yer whining. Yer no' a wean anymore."

Em scrambled back to her feet, her eyes watering with pain.

She could feel one shin bleeding inside her jeans. "Where are you taking me?" she demanded, trying to sound braver than she felt.

Could she get her hand into her pocket and reach her sketch pad? And if she did, what might she draw to free herself?

"Keep yer hands where I can see them," he said sharply. "I know about you lot and all yer sorcery. Ah'll no' stand for it on this island anymore." And he smacked her behind the knees with the long wooden stick he was carrying.

Em was feeling seriously scared now. Who was this man? How did he know about her abilities? About the abbey? More important, how had he managed to sneak up on her? She should have sensed his presence.

As her captor yanked her over the fence that bordered the public footpath, Em recognized him. He was one of the crofters who farmed the fields near the caves on Auchinmurn. A long time ago, a whole village of crofters had eked out a meager living from potato farming and raising sheep on the island. According to her grandfather, only one or two families still lived in the stone-and-peat cottages near the shore, mostly surviving on the occasional odd job and taking tourists on fishing trips. She'd spotted this one tending to a sheep tangled in a briar on the far side of the hill when she'd last sneaked up here. She'd thought he hadn't noticed her.

"I wasn't doing anything wrong," she said defiantly.

"That's not for you to say."

Em could smell the pipe tobacco in the top pocket of the crofter's tatty canvas field jacket. His cap was old, its mud-caked brim resting on bushy gray eyebrows. A front tooth was missing, and the others were yellow with black roots exposed. It gave him an ugly leer.

The only emotion Em could feel emanating from the crofter was a staunch resolve and a deep satisfaction. This worried Em more than if she had sensed terrible danger. The more she glanced at him in the moonlight, the more she could feel a drumming in the back of her head.

The last part of the climb down to the footpath was mostly on flat rock. The crofter slid down on his haunches, forcing Em to do the same.

"What have you been doing all these nights scratching away at them stones when ye should be in bed?"

So he'd been watching her. Now Em was truly worried.

"It's for a project," she mumbled, trying to keep herself from tumbling down the slope. She concentrated her imagination. Inspiriting the old man wouldn't hurt him. It would just calm him enough for her to wriggle free and get back to the abbey before anyone knew she was missing.

As she sent the first wave of calm toward him, a sharp pain stabbed behind her eyes. For a moment everything went black.

The next thing she knew, she was lying on the footpath, her hands and feet bound in plastic ties, feeling sick. This old man had somehow blocked her inspiriting powers.

The old crofter leaned on the fence marking the footpath and pulled a walkie-talkie from inside his jacket.

"I've got the lass," he said into the handset. "Aye, she's trussed up like a wild pig."

Em struggled to get back on her feet. The old man leaned over and cuffed her sharply behind the ear.

"Settle down."

Em was so shocked at being smacked that she didn't feel any pain for the first few seconds. Then her ear throbbed to life, hot and burning. The crofter tucked his crook under his arm, scooped her up, and threw her over his shoulder, carrying her along the footpath away from the abbey.

FIFTY-ONE

Tut-tut," Malcolm said smoothly. "None of that now, Mattie."

Matt's finger's felt sluggish. He couldn't draw. His father was stopping him . . . somehow . . .

Malcolm slipped his hand into his tunic and unrolled a parchment, revealing another of the old monk's bloody drawings. He waved it in the air, pacing back and forth, keeping a watchful eye on Solon, Matt, and Carik. "I have plenty of the old monk's drawings in reserve. He has been busy sketching all kinds of useful things for me," he said. He looked at Matt, taking a step closer. "I did so love building models when I was young like you, Mattie. One of my first was a reenactment of the great battle for Era Mina. There is a marvelous tapestry of the scene, hanging on the wall at the Royal Academy. I was quite inspired."

As quick as lightning, he slipped the parchment beneath the old monk's limp fingers.

A legion of ferocious miniature Viking warriors armed with long swords sparked into being, streaming from the machine, racing across the floor, swarming toward Matt. Carik screamed; Solon gasped.

"Their wee swords are tipped with poison," Malcolm added. "A nice touch, I thought. A recipe I learned from my mother."

Matt scrambled backward, stamping at the first wave of warriors. He caught and crunched several, their swords breaking with a satisfying snap under his boots. Carik and Solon dived in to help as Malcolm's laughter echoed around the chamber, but it was hopeless. More warriors followed, and more still, climbing the walls around Matt, hundreds and hundreds of them, their dragon helmets glowing in the darkness like the red eyes on a thousand roaches. Then they dropped en masse onto Matt's, Carik's, and Solon's bodies, stabbing at them as they fell.

Matt felt the world blacken. In his last moments of consciousness he saw his father tear up the parchment with bony fingers. The warriors blasted into a million pieces, leaving a splatter of blood soaking into the cavern floor.

When Matt regained consciousness, his head felt leaden, his chin pressing against his chest. He opened his eyes slowly.

What he saw shot panic into every limb and tightened every muscle.

His hands were bound in bloody half gloves and his head was locked in the iron mask. A fresh sheet of parchment lay fixed to a new wooden tablet before him. He was trapped inside the mechanical wraith.

Malcolm was standing in front of the cave drawing of the two-headed hellhound, observing him. Through the slit in the iron mask, Matt could see Solon and Carik slumped against the cave wall, looking pale and queasy.

"Awake at last," Malcolm said, sounding pleased. "We can proceed."

Matt had to stay in control of his imagination if he was going to survive.

"I won't help you!" he shouted. His voice boomed around his metal headpiece, deafening him. "I won't! You've done enough."

Malcolm scowled. Matt cried out, a nail of pain pounding into his forehead. Beneath the helmet his nose began to bleed.

"Have it your way," Malcolm said.

He unsheathed the bone quill from his belt. The quill's sharpened white tip glinted in the firelight, cold and deadly. Then he knelt in front of the old monk, now lying sprawled on the rock floor, and loosened his cowl, exposing his concave chest. Suddenly the bone quill looked less like a writing implement and more like a thin white dagger.

"Don't hurt him any more!" Solon choked, crawling across the dirt to lift the old man's head onto his lap.

Malcolm raised his eyebrows at Matt. "Will you cooperate or

not, Mattie?" Matt bit his lip so hard he could taste blood. He said nothing.

"I'll take that as a yes."

Malcolm left Solon cradling the old monk and strode over to the mechanical contraption. The animated knight who had formerly worked the machine had vanished when Malcolm tore up the last of the old monk's sketches. Malcolm took his place at the treadle.

With great difficulty Matt turned his head in the mask, to get a clearer view of Solon sitting bowed over his master. Brother Renard's eyes were cloudy and dim. His life was fading before Matt's eyes.

Matt thought of Jeannie still trapped in the tower. He had to do something soon to get her out of there, before she faced a similar fate.

Brother Renard stirred gently.

"Remember, my son," the old man whispered, gazing up at Solon. "Imagination is the real and the eternal. I failed to finish *The Book of Beasts*. Finish it for me, Solon. Finish . . ."

The rest of his words dropped into silence. He had gone.

With tears in his eyes and rage in his heart, Matt watched Solon kiss the old monk's forehead.

"Good-bye, master," he said.

Solon covered Brother Renard's face with the soft folds of the old man's cowl. Matt sensed Solon's fury. It jolted him from his own sadness. He struggled in vain against the straps binding his arms and feet. Solon was going to do something stupid, something rash that would achieve only more deaths, most likely their own.

Matt was about to plead with Solon to be careful, to think before he acted, when Carik took the young monk's shaking hands in hers. In seconds Solon's anger had dissolved. All Matt could sense now was a gut-twisting sadness.

FIFTY-TWO

Matt's neck was aching from the weight of the iron mask.

"What do you want from us?" he hissed at his father.

"You are a descendant of Albion, Mattie," Malcolm said conversationally. "With the bone quill, you have the ability to open this portal to Hollow Earth with my help. The only part of the puzzle that remains is the whereabouts of the manuscript you must copy from. *The Book of Beasts.* Then together, father and son, we can rule this world." Malcolm looked at Solon. "Where is the book?"

"You are full of madness and bile," snapped Carik.

Malcolm ignored her. "Where is the book, Solon?" he repeated.

Matt could sense telepathic messages flickering between Solon and Carik, but snagging them and deciphering them was impossible. To hear Em in his mind, all he'd ever had to do was listen to her imagination, to see its patterns of light. Then somehow in his mind, her thoughts became words that he could hear.

Oh, Em, thought Matt. *I wish you were here to help me.*

Perhaps if he did the same with Solon, he might hear something. He focused, but all he could hear was white noise.

"I don't know where the book is," Solon said, staring at Malcolm with hatred. "The abbot hid it. And as you have already killed him, its whereabouts may never be known."

Malcolm moved fast across the chamber and gripped Carik around her neck, lifting her off the ground, pressing her against the wall. Slowly but surely, he began to squeeze the life from her.

"Are you sure?" he said in a silky voice.

Matt tried to lift his hands to draw something on the parchment spread on the tablet before him, to help Solon and Carik, but the binding was too tight. His panic increased. He was beginning to hyperventilate. *Breathe slowly.* He had to find a way out of this mechanical monster. But how? He could hardly move his head, let alone the rest of his body.

Move your mind, son!

Matt froze. *Jeannie? Is that you?*

Jeannie's voice seemed to crackle through the static. *Move your mind . . .*

Jeannie! Jeannie! I don't know what you mean!

Matt was feeling light-headed with panic. He wished he'd paid more attention to Simon's lessons on inspiriting, on being a Guardian, on finding calm in a storm.

Closing his eyes, he took one deep breath, exhaled slowly, then another, and another, regulating his breathing, calming his mind and his palpitating heart.

Solon heard the last breath of air slowly hissing from Carik's lungs. Her face was beet red, her body limp beneath Malcolm's grip.

"Stop!" he said hopelessly, unable to bear it. "Please, stop! I . . . know where the book is hidden!"

Malcolm dropped Carik to the dirt, where she gulped and gasped for air. Solon helped her up, holding her close. He felt Malcolm's presence in his mind like a demon's claw scratching through his thoughts, uncovering the image of the abbot's throne chair.

"Fetch it for me," Malcolm commanded.

Solon held Carik more tightly. "It'll take me too long. My sister. The miller's family. They will perish if you don't release them first."

Malcolm looked unmoved. "No one is released until I have the book. Take that tunnel." He pointed to yawning rocky hole near the one they had dropped through only a short time ago. "It will bring you out above the bay. Your peryton will provide all the speed you need. Return the same way."

Solon glanced at Malcolm's infernal machine. Matt was slumped forward, as still as a statue.

Solon heard Carik's anxiety in his head.

I think he has gone.

What do you mean?

"Do not dawdle, boy," Malcolm growled. Black ink was dripping on to his chin in a thick blob. He wiped it with the back of his hand. "Fetch the book! Or I may not extend my mercy to your girl again."

Solon moved swiftly to the rope ladder and climbed back up the rock wall to the mouth of the tunnel Malcolm had indicated. Before he disappeared, he glanced again at Matt's motionless body.

Carik, do you think he's dead?

I sense nothing from him. Nothing at all.

FIFTY-THREE

Em did what she probably should have done the moment the old crofter had grabbed her. She called for help, deep inside her own mind.

Zach! Zach! Wake up. I need you right now!

The cottage the crofter had brought her to was made of flat stones insulated with thick dark peat, with a dark thatched roof. The thatch was tightly woven and, unlike the rest of the one-room cottage, not in need of repair. A large hearth took up most of the wall next to a row of high, small windows facing the sea. The windows were filthy, caked with salt and grime. The floor was made of the same stone as the walls and was as thick with muck as the windows. The place looked as if it hadn't seen a cleaning rag in years.

Against one wall was a wooden bed with a carved headboard that Em couldn't help staring at. It looked like a giant set of antlers. The bed was the only decent piece of furniture in the room, neatly made up with a fat red pillow and a windowpane quilt designed with the most vibrant colors and designs Em had ever seen.

Hundreds of books in every shape and size had been shoved in the cracks between the stones above and around the bed. Em felt such a rush of warmth from the strange library that she almost forgot that she'd been brought to this cottage against her will.

The rest of the room was sparse and unwelcoming. If it weren't for the books, the pot bubbling on the fire in the hearth, and the neatly made bed, Em would have thought no one had been here in weeks.

The crofter set a chair in the middle of the floor.

"Sit yerself on that," he said, and nudged her with his crook.

"Why can't I sit next to the fire?" Em said bravely. "I'm cold."

"I've heard what you weans did last time you were tied up. So sit yer arse on that chair. Now!"

Fear had seeped into the crofter's demeanor, and he was taking it out on Em. She sat on the chair.

Zach! Can you hear me?

No answer. Maybe she was too far from the abbey. Maybe he was in the deepest part of sleep. Em groaned. Why did teenage boys sleep so soundly?

The walkie-talkie on the mantel crackled to life. The crofter grabbed it and stepped outside, pulling the door closed behind him. Em stared up at the high windows. Even if she hadn't been tied up, she was too big to get through any of them. Besides, the crofter would probably return before she'd even reached them.

Em's blood ran cold as she considered the crofter's last words. *I've heard what you weans did last time you were tied up.* The last time she and Matt had been tied up and drawn their way out of trouble, they had been with two people she hadn't seen since, and very much hoped never to see again.

How did this old man know about it?

The walkie-talkie crackled outside the door. Em strained her ears but failed to hear the conversation. She and Matt had used walkie-talkies when they were younger, playing hide-and-seek in their old London flat. Walkie-talkies had a limited range, which meant whomever the old crofter was talking to was already on the island.

Em didn't have much time.

She hopped to the only front window and peeked outside. The old man was crouching beneath a tree, talking with his back to the door.

Em hopped back to the chair, leaning on it while she scanned the empty fireplace for a weapon. She rolled her hands against the plastic ties. Scissors would be nice. Or a knife. Then she stared at the ash on the hearth, and grinned.

Stay outside, old man. Stay outside.

Em sat down beside the hearth with her back to the fire. Without being able to see what she was doing, she began to sketch in the ashes.

FIFTY-FOUR

MIDDLE AGES

Jeannie was still fading in and out like a badly tuned radio station inside Matt's head. Matt concentrated, fixing her words in his mind as he heard them.

Call the grendel up from the center of the island. The grendel was the first beast to rise out of the muck an age ago, so it must be the last one bound away. You must possess it, control it. Hollow Earth will open to take it inside.

His hands were dirty. Clay lay under his nails and between his fingers from the cave floor when he had fallen beneath the poisoned weapons of Malcolm's tiny army.

Turning his head slightly, Matt could see Carik huddled in her corner again. Solon had gone. Malcolm sat in the corner of the cave, his arms hanging loosely on his knees, his head bowed, black liquid dripping from his mouth. Whether he was praying or sleeping, Matt did not know.

He worked at the clay stuck between his fingers, bringing it down to his fingertips. Then he lightly sketched the grendel on the corner of the parchment. Most of the image was hidden beneath his palm. He hoped the sketch was big enough.

He heard his mother's voice in his memory.

The power and longevity of any animation is affected by a combination of intent and imagination, Mattie. You have to will it to life.

Matt had never wanted to animate a drawing more.

When he had finished, there was no explosion of light anywhere in the cave. No lines of color leaped from his drawing. Nothing. Only a faint throbbing in the base of Matt's neck and a painful flash of light behind his eyes. He clenched his jaw to avoid letting out a yell.

Someone was beside him. He felt a cool hand on his arm.

"Carik?" he whispered, trying to turn his head to see her.

She squeezed his arm lightly, comforting him. "Despite leaving me in that cave, I'm at your service."

Malcolm's head shot up. His tongue flicked from the side of his mouth to catch a drop of inky blackness on its tip as his hand waved Carik back to her corner. Matt felt her unwillingness to go.

FIFTY-FIVE

Solon had no intention of retrieving *The Book of Beasts*, but he couldn't let the thought into his mind. If Malcolm sensed even an inkling of what he was planning to do, his sister and the others would suffocate in that terrible black swamp. Matt and Carik too were depending on him. He wouldn't let them down.

The moment Brother Renard had taken his last breath, Solon had made a promise that he would avenge his death. His and the abbot's. He accepted in his heart that he would have to break certain rules to achieve it.

The peryton's glimmer reflected like moonlight on the water as they soared together high above Era Mina. Solon gripped the peryton's antlers, doing his best to keep his plans locked safely away in his own mind until the right moment.

As the peryton soared to its highest point in the wispy clouds. Solon allowed a glimmer of his intentions to peep through.

In an instant the peryton had turned in midair and was heading straight downward again, toward the top of the pencil tower on the small island. The wind tore at Solon's cheeks. He wrapped his arms around the beast's neck, flattening his body across its back and tucking his head into its neck to prepare for the impact. The tower loomed in front of them. Solon closed his eyes and tightened his grip.

The peryton's massive antlers hit the tower like a battering ram, knocking a hole in the wall at the weakest point between the two topmost arrow slits. The momentum threw Solon off the peryton's back and onto the rubble in the heart of the shattered cell.

Jeannie lay on the straw, her head still weighted down by the mask. The peryton skidded to a stop near her head and sniffed her tenderly. She stirred, lifted her chained hand and patted the beast's nose.

"Ach, son," she slurred to Solon. "You shouldn't have come, but I'm glad ye did."

"Are you hurt, Lady Jeannie?" Solon asked, climbing out of the rubble and dusting himself down.

"I've been better." Jeannie shook her chains. "Would ye mind?"

Sorry, master, Solon thought.

Using the wall as his canvas, he etched a broadsword into the bricks with his dagger. He held his hand out to catch the sword's handle as it dropped from the air in a flash of silver.

Taking the sword in both hands, Solon hacked through the chains on the iron rings, freeing Jeannie from the wall. "I still need to break the iron clasp at the back of your mask," he warned. "It will cause discomfort."

"Do what ye have tae do, son. Don't fret about me."

Solon slammed the sword hilt into the pin on the clasp at the back of the mask, snapping it on his first try. He lifted the heavy iron casing gently off Jeannie's head and set it down.

Jeannie tugged Solon into a soft embrace, then turned her head back and forth, loosening her stiff neck muscles. "Thank you. Now where's oor Mattie?"

"Malcolm is holding him near the portal to Hollow Earth, in a painted cave inside the island," said Solon bitterly, helping her slide the iron cuffs from her wrists and ankles. "He has my friend Carik, too. Malcolm trapped my sister and others on Auchinmurn. They are in terrible danger, but he won't release them until I return with *The Book of Beasts*." He looked at Jeannie, willing her to understand. "I cannot give him the book. You must understand, too much is at stake. But I must save my sister somehow."

The peryton dipped its front legs and knelt next to Jeannie, who whispered into its pricked ears. The peryton snorted in response.

"You know where your sister and the others are?" Jeannie asked, gently brushing debris from the peryton's antlers.

Solon nodded.

"Then you take the beast and free yer sister and the others. Let me deal with Malcolm."

Solon flushed. "I cannot let an old woman fight a monster on her own."

Jeannie smiled kindly. "I will manage fine, son. My whole life, folks have been underestimating my abilities. I can handle Malcolm and he knows it. That's why he has kept me drugged and locked up here." She rolled her neck muscles again. "I'm feeling much better already. I've not eaten the food or water he sent with those two buffoons for a while. My imagination is as alert as ever."

The peryton snorted and dipped its forelegs again. Solon hesitated.

"Climb on, then," said Jeannie, giving him an encouraging push. "Let the beast help you. Then take your sister and the others to safety in one of the caves on the big island. Just in case."

Solon climbed slowly onto the peryton's broad back. "Just in case of what?" he asked, settling his sword at his side.

"Just in case my plan with Matt doesn't work and the beasts break free."

Matt trusted this woman. Solon decided he would trust her too.

FIFTY-SIX

PRESENT DAY

A hefty pair of scissors dropped out of nowhere above the hearth, hitting the floor with a loud smack. Em grabbed them and jumped back to the chair seconds before the old crofter clicked up the latch and stepped back inside, setting the silent walkie-talkie back on the mantel.

"Not long now," he said, folding his arms.

Em fiddled with the scissors behind her back, trying to position them so she could cut the plastic binding her wrists. It wasn't easy.

The crofter was staring curiously at her.

"Not long for what?" asked Em, maneuvering the scissors to her other hand.

"Not long for you to find a way to use the scissors you've animated to cut those ties."

He picked up the poker and scraped away the sketch in the ashy hearth.

Em's hands tingled as the scissors vanished in a burst of light. At least she'd managed to free her wrists from the chair.

"It was worth a try."

He laughed, a raspy smoker's laugh. "Ach, of course it was, lass. Yer just like yer father."

Through the front window, Em spotted two beams of light bouncing across the open field from the footpath. The fog had thickened considerably, making it look as if the flashlight bearers were floating toward the cottage. Friend or foe? She wondered.

The crofter smiled at the approaching lights.

Foe.

Adrenaline spiked through Em's system. She inhaled and exhaled slowly, keeping her emotions on an even keel. She needed to control her fears. If she was going to get away, she didn't need to contend with any additional obstacles from her imagination.

She tried to sense something more about this odd man than the same staunch resolve that she'd been detecting since he'd grabbed her at the stones. Again she felt a stabbing pain behind her eyes as he blocked her attempt at inspiriting him.

"Who are you?" asked Em, her skin tingling all over. "How do you know my dad?"

The beams of light were getting closer. Her best chance of escape was before whoever was carrying those flashlights made it to the door.

"Never mind who I am," the crofter said, pulling Em up from the seat. "Who *you* are is more important."

Em pushed up with her knees and slammed her head under the crofter's chin. His head whipped back and Em bit the edge of her tongue from the force. Lifting the chair with her free hand, Em slammed it down on the back of the crofter's head, knocking his cap off.

The chair was heavy and knocked the old man to his knees. But the blow hadn't been enough to knock him out. He rolled onto his back and grabbed for Em. Em scooped up some ashes from the hearth and threw them at the crofter's eyes. Grabbing the poker, she swung it against one of the crofter's knees. He howled in pain and crumpled to the ground again.

Momentum from the swing knocked Em off balance. Lunging at the mantel, she grabbed at the matches, knocking most across the hearth. Frantically, she reached for one of the matches on the mantel and tried to use it to draw an opening on the wall. The crofter leaped to his feet and yanked her backward, toppling them both to the floor. He wrapped his arms around Em and squeezed, his grip so tight around her chest that Em couldn't breathe.

She was going to pass out at any second.

FIFTY-SEVEN

MIDDLE AGES

The temperature inside the cave was dropping steadily. Carik was shivering, huddled against the far wall, but Matt's adrenaline was keeping his body temperature up despite the fact that Malcolm had stripped him of his coat before locking him into his machine. Matt's fingers were tingling; his feet had gone to sleep. The throbbing in his head was getting louder and beginning to worry him.

Could a healthy thirteen-year-old have a stroke?

Matt opened and closed his hands as best he could and wiggled his toes, forcing some circulation into his extremities. He peered through the slit in the iron mask at his father.

Malcolm had hardly moved since sending Solon to fetch the book. His arms hung loosely over his bent legs, as if he were about to pounce on his prey at any moment. His fingers seemed scalier and more clawlike than ever. Drops of inky liquid continued to ooze from the deformed side of his mouth, puddling in the dirt with a strange phosphorous glow. Malcolm was becoming the monster on the outside that he already was on the inside.

Matt watched his dad stir, his tongue flicking out into the air. It was thin and slick and forked, like a reptile's. He licked his fingers.

Without warning Malcolm sprang toward Carik, dragged her across the dirt, and dropped her in front of the carved mechanical monster.

"Don't hurt her!" Matt shouted, struggling in vain against his bindings. "Solon will bring you the book! He'll bring it!"

"He's been gone too long," Malcolm snarled. "I am starting to think he has abandoned you both to your fates."

"I don't care!" said Carik, scrambling away from Malcolm's reach.

Malcolm laughed, deep and throaty and animalistic. "You're a terrible liar, girl. You fear for his safety more than your own."

He casually seized Carik's wrist and squeezed. Matt watched as she struggled, slowed, and slumped over the clawed feet of the machine into a deep, inspirited sleep.

"My patience is wearing thin," Malcolm hissed. "We must begin soon."

FIFTY-EIGHT

The two figures that had burst into the cottage dropped their flashlights at the sight of Em and the crofter wrestling on the ground.

"Don't just stand there!" The crofter's guttural accent had changed, grown more refined. Em detected a gentle French accent. "Get her off me and secure her quickly!"

One of the figures grabbed Em and pulled her to her feet. Gasping, Em looked into a pair of cold green eyes.

Dressed in black with a stocking cap pulled low on his forehead, Tanan looked like a ninja warrior. Em recalled with a shudder how he had chased her and Matt through the caves on Era Mina over the summer. She couldn't even bring herself to look at Mara, who had once pretended to be their friend.

Surely the presence of such a powerful Guardian and two strong Animare would have triggered the abbey's defenses? It must at the very least have made an impression on Renard's imagination. It *must* have.

The crofter was pulling off his cap. The straggly wig came next, followed by the bushy eyebrows and the capped teeth.

Em knew at once who she was looking at.

A wave of terror washed over her, making her hands clammy and her chest tight. A dull, dizzying pain throbbed behind her eyes. Her grandmother Henrietta de Court was such a strong Guardian that her powers battered viciously at Em's mind. The firewall Renard kept around his own Guardian powers had never caused Em any pain. Henrietta de Court clearly didn't bother with such particulars.

In the shock of Em's realization, Tanan quickly and efficiently bound her hands again. Em screamed inside her head and out.

Zach! "Help! Mum!"

Before she could scream again, Tanan morphed into a demon right before her eyes. He rose up on thick haunches, every tendon and muscle on his body visible beneath a layer of reptilian scales, and gripped Em with long, sharp claws, his hairless head twitching, his tongue flicking. He had become the demon who had trapped her and Matt in the caves.

It was her own fear that had conjured Tanan as the demon again, Em knew. But it was still terrifying.

Get a grip, she admonished herself.

The demon flared its nostrils and then in a flash was human again. Tanan again. Em closed her mouth without another word.

"That's better," Tanan said. "Much easier for all concerned if you cooperate."

Em stomped down hard on his foot, then bucked upward, her head smacking into Tanan's chin. She enjoyed his yell of pain.

"Stupid girl!"

Cursing, Tanan tossed her onto the bed. Em swallowed back her tears. She would not let this man-demon see her cry.

Henrietta de Court loomed above Em now, studying her. Em could smell pipe smoke and a strange metallic odor.

"Why are you doing this?" Em whispered.

"Because you and your brother are an important part of a plan. A plan that will finally and forever allow we Guardians to control you Animare. No longer will we remain in service to your ridiculous aesthetic whims. It is time for *you* to serve *us*. Those Animare who help us achieve our new order will be rewarded handsomely and given positions of great importance." Her grandmother smiled coldly at Tanan and Mara.

Em wriggled, fighting hard against her bindings. "We'll do nothing to help you or your plan! Get away from me!" she yelled, pushing back against the wall so the sharp edges of the stones jabbed into her back.

Henrietta flicked a be-ringed hand. "Gloves, Tanan. We can't have her animating with her nails on that wall."

Tanan's clammy hands rolled gloves onto Em's bound hands.

Em exhaled slowly, calming herself. Doing her best to keep her fears at bay, to keep Henrietta out of her head.

Zach! Please, please wake up.

Silence.

Stay calm, she thought. *Focus.*

If help wasn't coming, she would have to help herself.

FIFTY-NINE

MIDDLE AGES

Jeannie watched until Solon and the peryton were a speck in the sky. Then she climbed down the rope ladder she had animated on the side of the pencil tower and stood for a moment on the beach, taking stock of her surroundings. The fresh air tasted good.

She set off around Era Mina, heading for the small island's north shore. She had not seen the caves on that side of the island since Matt, Em, and Zach had turned them into their hideout, but she had heard the details from Vaughn. Knowing Era Mina like the back of her hand, having spent her childhood and most of her adult life exploring it inside and out, Jeannie had chuckled to hear the twins and Zach plot and plan as if they were the first children to have ever explored the place.

That's as it should be, she thought. *Each generation discovering anew the ways of the past and adapting them to their own ends.*

Ignoring her arthritic hips, her swollen wrists, and all the screaming muscles in her body, Jeannie began her ascent of Era Mina's north face. The island's topography may have changed over the centuries, but its internal architecture was timeless. She knew this. Jeannie had sent the peryton to the cave opening at the cusp of this cliff to rescue Matt and Em once before. This time she would have to do the rescuing herself.

The opening to the caves was easier to access than she remembered, the ground cover and the bramble less dense and overgrown. Her limbs were trembling from exhaustion, and hunger was making her dizzy, but she had no time to stop and rest or eat. Tearing away the bushes, Jeannie animated a shovel and started to dig.

About ten minutes into her digging, a thunderous bellow erupted from Devil's Dyke on Auchinmurn opposite. The noise created an exodus of animals toward the shore and birds to the sky. A quake rippled across the hillside, knocking Jeannie, who was already weak, to the ground.

Matt had roused the grendel, just as she had told him to do.

Close to the peak and near the standing stones, the ground bulged like it was being inflated. There was a long chilling howl. Then, as if the air had been sucked from it, the bulge collapsed, leaving a sinkhole in the hillside. The grendel was moving underground and it was hungry.

Picking up her digging pace, Jeannie finally found the

opening to the cave of drawings. She cleared the clods of dirt and roots away from the hole and thought about shining a flashlight into the darkness to see how far the drop would be, but decided she couldn't risk alerting Malcolm to her presence. Feetfirst, Jeannie wriggled down into the chamber. She hoped she wasn't too late.

SIXTY

S he's too quiet," said Henrietta, sitting on the edge of the bed and touching Em's temple with one of her fingers.

Em recoiled. But she couldn't get away from her grandmother's hand. Her head felt terribly heavy and the headache was pounding much too loudly.

She was so tired.

"What are you plotting in that colorful little head of yours?" Henrietta mused.

"We won't help you," Em repeated stubbornly.

"I find that hard to believe," said her grandmother briskly. "You see, you have already helped us immensely. One might even say that all of this is down to you in the first place. Tanan? The tapestry."

Tanan dragged the tapestry, rolled in a heavy canvas tarp,

from its place against the back door. Then he unfolded a large
sheet of plastic and spread it across the stone floor. Together he
and Mara donned gloves and, slowly, and with great care, they
unrolled the bulky, fragile fabric. Then they knelt beside it with
an almost religious reverence.

The images on the tapestry sent a biting chill through every
part of Em's body. For a fleeting moment she was drowning and
she couldn't get a breath.

"Astounding, isn't it?" said Henrietta, clasping her hands
together in ecstasy.

Vaughn had told them Henrietta had stolen the tapestry. He
had even anticipated that the woven image had changed in some
way. But nothing could have prepared Em for this. She was looking at the same scene she had painted in the middle panel of her
triptych.

Like her painting, the tapestry depicted a central figure riding the black peryton, long hair covering part of his face. Em felt
more certain than ever that the figure was Malcolm. The peryton's tack was more detailed than she had painted it: a black face
plate studded in silver beneath the beast's blazing eyes, a red collar embroidered in gold with many of the mythical beasts that
Em recognized from the strange rings that had circled Era Mina
several days earlier. The peryton's saddle looked like flames were
licking across the red-and-gold fabric. Malcolm was clothed in the
same armor Em had painted, wings forged high on his shoulder
plates and the silver spiral on his chest.

In the tapestry, the hideous army of half-faced knights trailing behind Malcolm was captured in lush black and silver threads. The grendel dominated the narrative, its grotesque presence looming over the scene.

The worst section of the tapestry was the one Em could not bear to look at for more than a second. Matt lay slumped and bleeding, the bone quill jutting from the flesh above his hip.

"Why are you showing me this?" she choked out.

"Isn't it obvious?" said Henrietta, removing her gloves. "We need you to take us to Malcolm. We plan to help him finish his quest, and then we need you to return us to the present, where, in return for your help, you and your brother will be spared the same consequences as the rest of your family."

"I-I don't know of any way to get back to the Middle Ages," Em stuttered. "If I did, I would have returned for my brother before now."

"Ah," said Henrietta, "but I think you do. And if you choose not to tell me of your own volition, then I will have to persuade you."

The older woman's fingers pressed into Em's head, melding to her flesh and feeling their way into her imagination. Em screamed in anguish.

"Stop! Please!"

The pain was excruciating.

And then it wasn't.

SIXTY-ONE

E m was walking on the beach with the sun a blazing orange ball above rugged cliffs. The sea was calm and shimmering in the light. She waved at two boys dressed in rags, fishing off the shore in a rickety rowboat piled with nets. They looked curiously familiar. Em studied the landscape surrounding the bay, the high peaked cliffs, the tiny cove. This wasn't Auchinmurn.

Where was she?

Another stab of pain jolted her.

"My, she is a strong one," said Henrietta in surprise. "She must take after her grandfather. She's blocking me."

Em recognized the boys now. They were from Winslow Homer's painting *Boys Fishing, Gloucester Harbor*. The painting was in Renard's study, hanging near van Gogh's *Poppy Field*. Em remembered with a shock of excitement how she and Matt had projected themselves into *Poppy Field* when their grandfather was in a coma. She had clearly done something similar just now, fading into Homer's image to get away from Henrietta. Her mind rushed on in exciting leaps. If she could escape into *Boys Fishing* without even looking at it, what could she do with a picture of her own?

"I may have underestimated your abilities, Em, my dear," said Henrietta. "But do not underestimate mine. What are you planning?"

She put both hands on Em's head this time. The resulting pain scalded Em's temples for a moment. Then suddenly they felt soft and warm and comforting, and the pain disappeared. Em missed Matt so much. He was all alone, and so far, far away . . .

Em gulped at the air. "I won't tell you!"

Her chin dropped to her chest, her breathing slowed.

"Damn it! She's gone," said Henrietta, lifting her hand from Em's head. "I pushed too hard."

"She'll wake in time. Did you learn how she plans to travel back to the Middle Ages to fetch her brother?" Tanan asked eagerly.

Em remained still. It was important that Henrietta and the others believed her to be in a deep inspirited sleep. She detected anger emanating from her grandmother, but admiration too, and another oddly disconcerting emotion—pride in a job well done, in having somehow been responsible for her own granddaughter's considerable powers.

"Nothing yet," Henrietta said. "Watch her closely, Tanan. This is not over."

"Her hands are bound, Henrietta," said Tanan with a disbelieving laugh. "You've inspirited her. She's not going anywhere."

Em heard her grandmother snort with derision. "Tanan, you may be a powerful Animare, but sometimes you are a fool. She and her brother are unique. We do not fully know what they can do."

Em sensed her grandmother probing her mind again. She stiffened, but it was too late.

"Not sleeping after all?" inquired Henrietta, giving Em a cruel pinch. "Then let us continue. My son needs me and I will not let him down."

SIXTY-TWO

MIDDLE AGES

Malcolm dragged Carik away from the machine and dumped her in the corner beside the old monk's body. He pried Matt's fist open, shoving it away from the parchment. Matt's sketch of the grendel was visibly throbbing.

"It's not an animation," Matt said defiantly as his father made to snatch the parchment from the machine. "I've summoned it. It's coming to get you whether you tear that up or not."

"You stupid boy!" he roared, spitting globs of ink onto his chin and neck. "What have you done?"

"Exactly what Jeannie told me to do," snapped Matt, his voice muffled behind the mask.

Malcolm slapped his hand on the side of the mask in fury, bouncing Matt's forehead against the unyielding metal. "Then you will draw something else to fight it for me."

He put a fresh piece of parchment in the machine, shoved a piece of charcoal between Matt's fingers, and hurried around the wooden machine and stepped onto the treadle.

The iron glove prevented Matt from throwing the charcoal away. The gears began to grind, the belts and pulleys stretching and turning as the machine sparked to life. With Malcolm's first few steps, Matt didn't feel anything. But as his father walked faster, Matt's fingers curled against the charcoal, his skin tight and on fire. He could feel his father's malevolence worming into his thoughts.

Matt bit back the pain, the burning sensation spreading up his arms. He felt as if he were being immersed in boiling water. His dad's presence in his head was overpowering. Malcolm was pushing an image into Matt's mind, and Matt could no longer block it.

At first the image was merely a silhouette, a black-and-white outline of a beast. Then the image fattened and fleshed out. Its hindquarters became the thick haunches of a lion and a tail as thick as a cable. Its head and chest grew into the body of a majestic eagle, its wings tipped with white, its eyes blazing green.

"The griffin is one of the guardian beasts of Hollow Earth," snarled Malcolm, his movements on the treadle becoming erratic. "It will fight for us. Animate the griffin or the girl will truly suffer!"

Matt couldn't stop himself. The iron glove creaked and groaned as he sketched the bottom half of the griffin, then its wings, and finally its head with its ferocious hooked beak. But before he could bring it to life, a rumbling shook the chamber and a stench worse than rotting meat bled through the walls.

With a crash the grendel—the death-eater, the mud-monster—entered the chamber, smashing through the rock as easily as if it were made of paper. Its boneless, hulking, stinking shape began sucking hungrily toward them. Carik woke, screamed, and scrambled across the rocky floor to take shelter behind the wooden machine.

Malcolm was galloping on the treadle now. "Faster!" he screamed. "Faster!"

Matt felt as if he was suffocating from the pain. His hand was moving in a blur. The griffin was taking shape, filling in and flexing its wings.

The grendel's apelike head scanned its surroundings. It raised its nostrils into the air, scenting death. Lumbering across the chamber, it hovered over the old monk. Matt watched, paralyzed with horror, as the beast sucked out old Brother Renard's heart, then spilled its thick, muddy torso over the old man's body and absorbed the rest of his flesh.

Behind him Matt could hear Carik slipping her knife from the strap at her ankle. With the little strength he had left, he whispered:

"Don't, Carik. I know what I'm doing, and I need that monster to do it."

He heard the slow sheathing of the knife again, and exhaled. If he could just stop drawing the griffin . . . One monster he could handle. Two, he wasn't so sure.

At that moment, Jeannie dropped into the cave screaming like a banshee.

"Malcolm Renard Calder, release those weans or I'll make you feel pain like you've never felt before!"

Malcolm stumbled in shock and slipped from the treadle. Matt's fingers slowed and stopped as Jeannie advanced across the cavern.

"Yer schemes will come to naught, son," she warned. "Stop all of this and I can help ye make good the damage."

"This isn't damage!" Malcolm screamed. "This is my destiny!"

He threw himself in fury at Jeannie, but she was expecting his attack and dodged out of his way. Carik's knife flashed from its sheath again as, stumbling and roaring, Malcolm bore down on Jeannie once more.

The grendel snuffed the air and roared, filling the cavern with foul air, its oozing body threshing from side to side in search of a fresh victim. There was just was one more thing Matt needed to do.

Control the beast, son. You can do it.

Matt spat on the parchment and erased the grendel's eyes. In their place, he imagined his own.

SIXTY-THREE

All at once Matt's perspective fractured, as if he were looking through the thick glass bottom of a bottle. He saw himself, lashed to the foul machine. He saw Jeannie and Malcolm weaving from side to side, Carik's knife poised and ready to slash. He had done it. He was the grendel.

He looked down at the corpulent mass of festering muck that was the grendel's body. Across the cavern he saw his human body gagging, and he tasted bile. The grendel was a conflagration of millions of sucking, faceless mouths, like flames licking out from the thick black sludge. Matt felt them all pressing in on him. Swallowing his disgust, he urged the beast forward, controlling its will . . . controlling its hunger.

The grendel lumbered toward Malcolm, who stood defiantly

in front of Jeannie, his eyes darting between Matt's empty eyes and the monster's ravenous ones.

"Very clever, Mattie. I knew you wouldn't disappoint. Your abilities are beyond what I ever could have imagined."

The grendel moved closer. Malcolm stepped back. "Mattie, think about what we could achieve together, you and I? Father and son."

Matt heard his father's words as if he were underwater. This man in front of him, this abomination, was no longer his father. Never really had been.

"Lass," Jeannie said to Carik, "help me get Matt out of this contraption. Then ye must leave. Any minute now, a whole world of terrible is going to break open, and I'd like you not to be here when that happens."

"I'm not leaving," said Carik at once as she helped Jeannie wrench open the locks binding Matt's ankles and feet, tearing the vile metal gloves from his fingers. "I can fight."

"This isn't yer battle, lass," said Jeannie.

Controlling the grendel, keeping Malcolm pinned in the corner of the cavern, was draining Matt of everything he had.

"Jeannie, I feel sick," he whispered. "I don't know how long I can do this."

Jeannie's hand squeezed his own. "Not much longer, son. Promise."

Matt felt the smash of something heavy breaking open the clasp on his iron mask, the blessed relief of air on his face.

Still he held the grendel's mind and watched Malcolm with the grendel's eyes.

"Go," Jeannie ordered Carik.

Carik glowered. "I will not—"

"I need you to trust me, lass. If you don't leave now and join Solon, there will be no future for Matt or his sister."

Matt's head was spitting open. The grendel's bloodlust was strong. He could feel how much it wanted to rip Malcolm apart. How much longer could he keep control?

He suddenly felt Carik's cool hand on his. "You have my pledge forever, Matt of Calder."

Matt's voice felt unsteady. He had grown fond of the fierce Viking girl. "And you have mine. You and Solon. For what it's worth."

"Climb up through that hole and ye'll find yerself out on the hillside, lass," Jeannie instructed, guiding Carik away from the foul, stinking slime of the growling grendel. "The North Star will be high on your right side. Find yer way to the mill, where Solon is waiting for you."

Matt's concentration had slipped as Carik looked into his eyes—the grendel's eyes—in farewell.

It was a mistake.

Carik's eyes suddenly widened. "Look out!"

Her warning was too late. Matt felt a piercing agony in his side.

His father had plunged the sharp white tip of the bone quill deep into his own son's flesh.

SIXTY-FOUR

Zach woke up with a hollow silence in his head and a really bad feeling in his gut. His clock read 4:20 a.m. It was still dark outside and would be for a few more hours, but his stomach was doing somersaults and he tasted salt in his mouth.

He burped. His stomach rumbled. His gut twisted. Throwing off his duvet, he dashed across the hall to the bathroom.

Oh, man, he thought, holding his hand to his mouth. *Sandie must not be allowed near the stove anymore.*

Since Jeannie's absence, Sandie had decided that it was her responsibility to cook for everyone and insisted that Renard not replace Jeannie with anyone else. They didn't need any strangers in the house at this time. This was the second night in a row that Zach had woken up with an ugly stomachache.

He flushed the toilet, then quickly brushed his teeth, staring at himself in the mirror. His short blond hair stood up in spikes and the skin under his hazel eyes was puffy. He spat, rinsed, and splashed water on his face.

He was hardly back in his bedroom when his gut clenched again. The taste in his mouth was stewed cabbage. He moaned and headed back to the bathroom, glancing absently at Em's bedroom door as he passed. It was open. He could see from here that her bed was empty.

And then it hit him.

What if it wasn't Sandie's burgers that had woken him? What if it was Em? What if she was wandering outside again and was now in trouble?

Ever since he had met her, Zach had felt Em's presence in his head. A soft purple wrapped around his thoughts, a wisp of pale violet cushioning his ideas, a pale light always in his mind.

Standing in the hallway in his boxers, Zach closed his eyes and listened for her. Nothing except a dull emptiness that he'd blamed on Sandie's cooking.

Yanking on a T-shirt, thick checked shirt, and jeans, Zach ran into Em's empty bedroom, doing his best to keep the rising panic at bay.

Em! Can you hear me?

Nothing.

He closed the door and turned on the light. Then he sat on her bed and looked around. The room was not only void of her presence, but she had been gone for a while. The only sense of Em was emanating in a barely visible blue aura from her three-paneled comic strip of the warrior princess, lying open on her desk. The princess looked ferocious, a lot like Em. Zach threw off the memory of their recent encounter with the princess's arrows at the abbey gates.

All the other posters and prints of her favorite comic-book characters and the shelves of her books were still. Usually Em's imagination kept everything around her perpetually pulsing, almost alive.

Zach switched off the lamp, pulled open the curtains, and let a shaft of moonlight illuminate the room. He could sense things better in the darkness.

Almost at once he was aware of something significant.

Since Matt had disappeared, Em had taken to wearing one of his hoodies all the time. Last night the hoodie had been over the back of her desk chair. Not anymore.

Zach did a quick search of her laundry basket. As he did, Em's scent hit him hard. He slammed the lid on the basket and sat on it for a few minutes until he felt he was back in control of himself. The hoodie wasn't there.

Em? Where are you?

White noise buzzed in his head.

SIXTY-FIVE

Middle Ages

Matt was dimly aware of a howl of horror. His grip on the grendel's mind was loosening, and his eyes couldn't focus and his head felt cloudy. He looked up at Jeannie and Carik from his own body. He could feel the wound directly above his hip bone, deep and bleeding profusely.

"It is bad?" he mumbled.

Jeannie snatched Carik's knife and charged at Malcolm.

"Yer own flesh and blood, Malcolm! How could you?"

Malcolm whipped his plated arm at her head. Jeannie dropped to the left and took the brunt of the attack on her shoulder. She gasped, but didn't slow down.

"You heard the boy. He has no use for me," Malcolm snarled. "We could have ruled the world, but he turned my glory down."

Jeannie thrust herself forward, the knife blade aimed for Malcolm's heart.

Matt could feel himself fading. There was noise. Howling. Shouting. The sound of feet dropping to the cave floor and a familiar voice. He struggled to stay awake, but it was hard. His side felt as if it were on fire. Blood was dripping through his fingers. The grendel was shaking free of his control.

Solon's sword was sharp and swift, sweeping with deadly accuracy. Malcolm's head toppled to the cave floor. Carik made an inarticulate noise and ran to Solon, throwing herself into his arms and kissing him fiercely.

Jeannie was with Matt again, checking his wound. "Son? Speak to me."

"Still . . . here," Matt whispered.

Solon knelt next to Matt.

"Your sister?" Matt asked.

"She and the others are safe." Solon slipped a folio from under his tunic. "Take it. Use it. End this."

Matt pulled himself up against the cavern wall. He ran his fingers over the manuscript. He held *The Book of Beasts* at last.

Only a few feet away, the grendel seemed fascinated with Malcolm's severed head. Matt wanted to close his eyes but couldn't.

"Keep your eyes and your imagination with the grendel," Jeannie coaxed. "We must be able to control it, or we will never take it through the portal. And we must do that, Mattie. We must put the last beast in with its kind, into Hollow Earth forever."

"I can do that," croaked Matt, doing his best to disguise his pain with a weak grin.

"I have faith in you." Jeannie leaned closer. "Son, I'm so sorry but this is going tae hurt."

Before Matt had a chance to prepare himself, Jeannie yanked the bone quill from his side and placed it in Matt's hands. The pain was blinding. There was a ripping sound as Jeannie tore a piece of fabric from her blouse and packed it into the wound.

Hundreds of smoky tendrils with gaping mouths swarmed over Malcolm's body as the grendel sucked blindly at Malcolm's engorged heart. Seconds later only bones remained on the cave floor. Matt knew his dad had become something ugly, a festering monster riddled with hate. But he couldn't help himself. Tears streamed down his cheeks.

"Mattie, son, can ye hear me?" Jeannie said gently.

Matt swallowed and nodded.

"You're doing fine, son. Stay with me."

Jeannie turned to Solon and Carik. "Take care of yourselves," she said. "Find a way to heal these islands."

"I hope we meet again sometime," Matt told Solon and Carik. It was an effort to speak. "Thanks for helping me, both of you."

"Now scat," said Jeannie with a smile.

Solon and Carik left the cavern. Matt felt their loss immediately.

The stench from the grendel filled the cave with a sickening mustard fog as its hunger swept toward Jeannie. It began to move.

"We have to open Hollow Earth right now, Jeannie," whispered Matt. "I want to go home."

Jeannie squeezed his hand. "Then draw the grendel, son. Draw, like our lives depend on it."

Matt knew that they did.

Matt released the grendel from his mind. Swiftly he turned his eyes to the manuscript page and began to draw.

The grendel lurched forward and touched the etching of the hellhound with the shapeless tip of its bloodied nose. At its touch the hellhound's heads snapped forward. Its paws tore from the wall as it hurled itself out of the drawing, straight into the wide, sucking mouth of the grendel.

A great silver helix spun slowly against the cavern wall where the hellhound had leaped from the stone. It was rotating, getting faster, sending blinding ribbons of light out into the cavern.

"Ready, Mattie?" said Jeannie.

Matt pictured his family, sitting around a roaring fire at the Abbey. He was going home. Somehow.

"Born ready," he said.

The grendel seemed calm now, as if it knew where it was going. It needed only the smallest nudge to put its head up against the spinning helix. The helix flexed and widened, pulsing like a great white heart, enveloping the monster.

Jeannie took Matt's right hand as he finished the drawing. "Now!" she cried.

Matt and Jeannie stepped into the silver light.

SIXTY-SIX

PRESENT DAY

Zach searched for Em in every room on the children's floor of the abbey as carefully and quietly as he could. He trusted that his movements were stealthy, and that he was opening and closing doors without much sound. He also knew from nights when he and Matt would sneak into the kitchen for slices of pizza or Jeannie's cake which floorboards on the abbey's back staircase squeaked.

After a fruitless hunt in the kitchen, he moved across the foyer and into the library. Maybe she'd fallen asleep reading. It wouldn't be the first time.

He had taken only a few steps into the room when an intense pulse of light exploded in his brain, dropping him to his knees. He squeezed his eyes against the pain and gagged at the taste of salt and seaweed in his mouth as the vision flickered in front of his eyes.

Em was holding the reins of a gilded seahorse as she drove a golden chariot across the bay. She was dressed like a warrior in silver chain mail, a steel-gray breastplate, and a purple cape that matched the streak in her hair. A quiver of arrows hung from her shoulder. The cape was veined with threads of silver, and billowed out behind the ethereal-looking chariot. An army of smaller but equally resplendent seahorses in a rainbow of colors followed behind her.

The image disappeared in a flash, leaving Zach on the library floor with floaters dancing in front of his eyes. His nose was bleeding.

Wiping the blood with the hem of his T-shirt, he got to his feet and bolted from the library. He didn't care about the pounding at the base of his skull or the blood at the back of his throat. He could sense Em at last. His mind was awash in her pale violet light.

He knew exactly where he'd find her.

Zach burst back into Em's bedroom, skidding across the sopping-wet floor. Em was soaked and shivering, lying in the fetal position directly beneath the pulsing image of her comic-book drawing.

Zach gazed once again at the center image of the warrior princess riding across the waves on her golden chariot. It was still pulsing with the energy and light from an animation.

Grabbing a blanket from the back of the couch in the sitting room, he stripped Matt's soaked hoodie from Em's body and wrapped her in the soft blanket. He was about to toss the hoodie aside when Em's eyes snapped open.

"No!" she cried, grabbing it from Zach's hand and pressing its soggy folds to her chest.

Shh, Em. It's okay. It's going to be okay.

Zach pulled her close as she shivered and cried, wrapping her tightly in his arms and sending calm and soothing thoughts into her mind. Em relaxed against him at last.

For a while they sat together on the floor of the sitting room, saying and thinking nothing. Zach pulled a handful of long, sparkling silver threads from Em's hair. When he brushed them to the ground, they sparked and fizzled, then disappeared.

Em opened her eyes and smiled up at him sleepily.

Hey.

Hey to you, too. What happened? Where have you been?

Oh, Zach, I'm so happy to see you.

She lifted her hand and touched his chin, sending a jolt of electricity through him. He tugged out a fresh silvery strand from her hair and held it before her eyes.

You fell out of your own comic book?

Em sat up, pulling the blanket tighter around her body, the light of memory in her eyes. She looked around the room at her familiar belongings. *I just . . . imagined myself into it. And now I'm here. With you.*

She smiled exultantly at Zach. As her intense feeling of accomplishment flooded his mind, Zach returned her smile. It was impossible not to. Then he pulled her into a hug.

He pushed her away again almost at once.

Jeez, Em, you're burning up. I need to get your mum.

Em's teeth had started chattering. *It's the effort of animating by imagination. I'll be fine. I just need to . . . sleep . . .*

Her eyes rolled under her eyelids and she passed out.

SIXTY-SEVEN

Henrietta de Court did not like to lose.

"*Bon dieu!*" she hissed in rage, staring at the space where, moments earlier, Em had been lying. "You could not think of one thing to animate that might have kept her here?"

Tanan scowled in response, rubbing at the welt on the side of his face where Henrietta had slapped him.

"And *you*," Henrietta spat, whirling around to Mara. "What about you? Useless, the pair of you. Now my granddaughter is gone and we have no means of returning to the past to help my son! I should have gotten rid of you both, years ago, the last time we had this kind of trouble."

"You need us," Tanan said sullenly. "You can't draw the way we can."

Henrietta pursed her lips. He was right.

"There now, my dears," she said, altering her tone. She smoothed Mara's long, silky hair from her face and wiped the tears from her cheeks. "Let us say no more of this. We will simply retrieve Emily and begin again."

Mara seemed grateful for the reprieve. Tanan remained watchful. Henrietta admired Tanan's ambition almost as much as his skill as an Animare, but she sensed that when Malcolm returned, he might not be so pliable. She did not have the strength to keep him under control for the rest of her life. When the time came, she would seriously have to consider which Animare was the most use to her.

"Em has undoubtedly alerted the abbey to our whereabouts," she said briskly. "So the first thing we must do is abandon this charming abode."

"And then what?" asked Tanan.

"And then we watch, we wait, and we try again."

"If we couldn't convince the girl to bend to our will this time, then what makes you think we'll be more successful a second time?" Tanan demanded. "Renard and Sandie won't let her out of their sight when they find out what happened. Add Vaughn and Simon to her own private security team, and we may not get another chance."

Henrietta tipped out the contents of Em's backpack, which had remained on the bed where Em had left it. A flashlight, a sketch pad, two nubby pencils, balled-up tissues, a KitKat bar, a photograph of Matt, and bag full of scrapings from the stones at Devil's Dyke. Henrietta looked at the photograph of Matt first.

"He is his father's double," she said, smoothing the picture out with her thumb. "Such a handsome boy." Slipping the photograph into her pocket, she picked up the bag of scrapings next, turning it over in her hand. "What are you up to, *ma biche?*" she said thoughtfully.

She stared at the bag for a while longer before returning it and the other items to Em's pack.

"Do you have something?" said Tanan, watching the expression on Henrietta's face.

Henrietta smiled. "I believe Emily will take us to Malcolm after all."

She pulled on the crofter's tweed jacket and headed for the door.

"Where are we going?" said Mara, quickly dousing the fire. Tanan rolled the tapestry and hoisted it over his shoulder.

"Era Mina," said Henrietta, stepping out into the chill of the night. The moon was dark, hidden behind a veil of clouds. "Tanan, *cherche pour nous un bâteau.* A boat. And I need a warm coat. Fur."

SIXTY-EIGHT

Em's vital signs were strong and she would make a full recovery. The adults had gathered in the library now, and were standing in a row, looking at Zach with the air of wartime interrogators.

Zach decided to preempt them.

"What do you want to know?" he signed wearily.

"Everything," said Sandie at once. "Where has Em been? What has been happening?"

"I'm still puzzling the details out for myself," Zach admitted. "But I think she went out by herself earlier and got into some kind of trouble. To escape, she imagined herself into her comic-book drawing. Then she fell out of the picture and into her room. That's where I found her. That's what she said."

"Well, I'll be damned," said Vaughn in wonder. "She's figured out how to fade. Took me years of training to access my imagination in that way, and she did it without any practice into one of her own paintings. Outstanding!"

Sandie glared at Vaughn. "There's nothing *outstanding* about my daughter putting herself in mortal danger."

"What else, Zach?" prodded Simon. "What's Em been up to? She's been very secretive lately."

"Does it have something to do with Jeannie's shed?" Sandie added, glancing at Vaughn. "Vaughn and I saw you both heading that way the other night."

Zach hesitated. Em had sworn him to secrecy about the painting in Jeannie's shed. Could he break his promise?

He felt the vibrations as Simon angrily banged the library table. "No more secrets! Em's life . . . *Matt's and Jeannie's* lives depend on this."

"We know Henrietta is on the island," Vaughn signed from the window. "It's unlikely she's here alone. My guess is that Tanan may be with her. Maybe Mara, too. Is that where Em has been? Henrietta de Court would love to put Em's talents to use."

Vaughn was the least efficient among them at sign language since he had not spent as much time at the abbey with Zach as the others. He spelled out his words more slowly, pausing at odd places in his sentences. This usually made Zach smile. Not tonight.

Zach slowly exhaled. "I don't know whether Em's been with Henrietta or not. All I know is that she's created a painting," he signed. "A triptych. She painted it over the medieval picture of Daniel in the lions' den that used to hang in the library."

"I liked that painting," said Renard with a frown.

"Why use an existing painting?" asked Simon.

"She wanted materials that would have been available in the Middle Ages to create what she needed. Roots and honey for paint, among other things." Zach thought of the roadkill hanging in the shed. "She's been having visits from a ghost, a spirit she thinks is Albion. She thinks he's telling her to paint the things he's shown her, and then use the painting to rescue Matt."

Renard inhaled sharply. "The last time Albion appeared, it was to Duncan Fox. We know from Fox's diaries that he painted the cave mouth to Hollow Earth shortly after that surreal visit."

"Em included a copy of Duncan Fox's painting in her triptych," Zach signed, remembering.

Simon shook his head. "Creating an authentic work in order to travel in time? I'm not sure that's possible, no matter how brilliant the Animare."

"Why not?" signed Zach. "Matt and Em are unique. Who knows what they'll do next?"

"I agree with Zach," said Vaughn. "We don't even have a name for the kind of combined Animare and Guardian powers that are evolving in the twins."

Sandie stood up angrily. "I have names for them. Matt and Emily. They're my children. What *matters* is looking after Em and nursing her back to full strength. What *matters* is bringing Matt and Jeannie home."

"When Em wakes up, she can tell us about Albion herself," said Vaughn, resting his hand on Sandie's shoulder. "If Em is experiencing leaps in her abilities, then Matt may be too. He may already be on his way home."

Sandie smiled gratefully at Vaughn, setting her hand on top of his.

"Show us the painting, Zach," signed Renard. "When Em wakes up, we'll decide what to do. But we'll decide together."

PART THREE

PART THREE

SIXTY-NINE

Vaughn stood in front of Em's triptych, which had been set up in the library. He looked like he was deep in contemplation. Em bit her lip, wondering what he was thinking. Was traveling back in time via the painting to rescue Matt a stupid idea?

She had been angry with Zach at first, for breaking his promise and telling the adults her plan. But remembering her helplessness at the hands of Henrietta, a part of her was glad, too. She had told the adults everything that had happened to her in the cottage, in the knowledge that she wouldn't be alone this time.

"The impressions you've captured of this unfinished battle, Em," Vaughn said at last, tracing the images of Malcolm and the knights and the grendel. "It reminds me of the battle depicted in the Royal Academy tapestry that Henrietta stole."

Renard grunted in agreement. "The details are different, but the image is much the same," he agreed. "You saw the tapestry at the cottage, Em. Does it now show this scene instead of the original?"

Em remembered the ghastly beauty of the tapestry that Tanan had unrolled in the crofter's cottage. She had been struck by the similarities, too. "It's almost exactly the same," she said.

"A possible past," said Simon a little grimly. "Malcolm in victory, conquering the grendel."

"Possible but not yet fixed in history," Renard said. "Remember, time isn't linear."

"Concentric circles," said Em, remembering the whirling lights above Era Mina, and the helix.

"If the tapestry has changed again, Henrietta will know," said Sandie.

"Not necessarily," Zach signed. He looked at Em. "You said they had to unroll it? Maybe they rolled it up again. Maybe now Matt's the one standing in victory at the center, but no one knows that yet."

Em smiled at Zach, feeling better at this thought.

"Can you sense Henrietta's presence, Grandpa?" asked Em.

"I know she's close, but nothing more specific than that," Renard said. "Henrietta is skilled at masking her mind. If she has Tanan and Mara to help her, then she may have also masked her physical presence in some way. But let us worry about that."

"We should eat," said Sandie. "There's macaroni and cheese, if you can face it. I burned the top, I'm afraid."

"That's why ketchup was invented," said Vaughn, earning a cuff on the shoulder.

Everyone turned away from the tall windows and headed to the kitchen. They missed the brief frizz of electricity spidering over the bay outside, revealing for one brief moment the animated blue outline of a sleek yacht bobbing on the water. It was gone again in an instant.

Inside the large and comfortable cruiser, Henrietta was preparing dinner in the yacht's galley. She squeezed a fresh lime into a mixing bowl, added chopped garlic and crushed red peppers, and blended the ingredients well. Touching her finger to the cloudy liquid, she lifted a droplet to her lips. Perfect to mask the taste of the valerian root she had been feeding Mara and Tanan for the past few days. It had only had a slight soporific effect on Tanan so far, but Mara was already beginning to think she was ill. Today's dose, added to what had accumulated in their systems to date, would be enough to take care of Mara at least.

Reaching into a bag on the narrow counter, she lifted out a small plastic box containing a dark green root. She cut two thin slices and chopped them finely, scraping them with the back of the knife into her lime marinade. Finally she drizzled the poisoned marinade over two of the shrimp skewers and popped them under the grill.

She looked out through a porthole at the monk's tower dominating the beach on this side of Era Mina. Then her gaze passed across the water to the grounds opposite, the jetty and the lawn of the abbey itself. The lights were on in the library, but there was no one inside. The powerful binoculars Mara had animated earlier had shown Henrietta that Em and the others had retired to the kitchen.

The timer beeped on the grill. Henrietta slid the shrimp from their skewers onto plates already prepared with a salad, which she carried from the galley to the table in the spacious, well-appointed cabin.

"How long will we have to wait here?" asked Tanan moodily, pouring himself a glass of red wine.

"Not long now," said Henrietta, lifting her glass. "*Salut.*"

Tanan and Mara held their glasses aloft. Mara's hand was a little shaky.

"To our sons and daughters," said Henrietta, smiling benevolently at her co-conspirators. "Never forget imagination is the real and the eternal."

"This is Hollow Earth," replied the others.

Mara clinked glasses with Tanan and gulped her wine.

Before she could finish her salad she was dead.

SEVENTY

Three Animare will be better equipped to face Hollow Earth,"
said Renard. "Vaughn and Sandie, you'll go on this journey
with Em. I think Simon needs to stay here and help guard the
abbey with me. Henrietta is still out there, and likely knows we're
planning something."

"I'm going too," Zach signed stubbornly.

Renard glanced at Simon, who nodded. "Fine," he said. "Four
of you, then."

Em felt an intense wave of relief. She couldn't imagine facing
this unknown without Zach at her side.

"What if this doesn't work?" she said, feeling a little desperate.

Vaughn pulled on his dark flak jacket, filling the pockets with chalk, charcoal, crayons, and paper. "If we can't fade through your painting, then we try something else," he said, and patted his pockets. "But I think we'll be fine."

"And Albion will help," added Renard, pulling Em into a hug. "Somehow."

Em dressed quickly in black leggings, her favorite knee-high black boots with thick black socks for extra warmth, a long-sleeved T-shirt, and one of Matt's black hoodies under her jacket. Vaughn and Sandie were also in black.

Sandie offered Em a stocking cap. "Want this?"

"I'm fine," said Em, and zipped her hoodie up to her chin.

But she wasn't. What if she had misunderstood Albion's intentions?

I'll be there, Zach reminded her, smiling into her eyes.

They gathered at the end of the jetty, waiting for Renard to reverse the boat from the boathouse. Simon and Zach wrapped Em's triptych in tarpaulin and lifted it carefully aboard. Em climbed onto the boat with Vaughn and Sandie, holding tightly to her mother's hand. Then Simon took the helm with Renard, and steered them all across the bay to Era Mina.

The island had lost most of its trees many years earlier. To Em it looked even more barren than usual as they sailed west to Monk's Cove, on the northwest side of the island.

Simon and Renard moored the boat next to two stout rocks, and helped the others ashore with Em's painting.

"Are you sure we shouldn't have left the painting in the

library?" said Renard anxiously. "You would return directly to the abbey that way."

Em shook her head. "We know the island has its own power. We might need all Era Mina to make it work. That's why we're taking it with us."

She gazed around the cove, remembering the stiff climb up the cliff face to access the caves inside the island. She, Matt, and Zach had made the climb many times that summer. It seemed a long time ago.

Sandie and Zach hugged Simon and Renard good-bye, and joined Em and Vaughn at the foot of the cliff.

"Ready?" said Vaughn beside Em, shouldering the triptych in its tarpaulin.

Em ran back to her grandfather, who swept her into a hug. The feeling of his arms was like a cozy blanket, and she had to laugh.

"You make me feel so warm and safe," she said, gazing up into Renard's much-loved face.

"It's the least I can do," he said. "Now go. Be brave, and bring your brother and Jeannie home. Simon and I will be waiting."

Em ran back the others waiting for her at the foot of the cliff, pausing only to blow Simon and Renard kisses. Renard caught his and placed it against his heart.

SEVENTY-ONE

Henrietta watched from the cabin window through her binoculars, tracking the boat until it disappeared around the south coast of Era Mina.

"The game's afoot," she said with satisfaction. "They will enter Hollow Earth tonight, I am sure of it. And I will be with them. Then my son will come home, bringing glory and power with him."

"What do you want to do with her?" said Tanan, nudging Mara's motionless body with his foot as he stood up. He seemed uninterested in how or why she had died.

It is just as well, Henrietta thought with some amusement. *As you will soon join her.*

"Unless you object," she said aloud, "I'd suggest over the side."

"Why would I object?"

"I wondered whether you had a soft spot for her," said Henrietta.

Tanan's gaze was steady. "I care for nothing but Hollow Earth and Malcolm's vision for us all."

"Then what are we waiting for?" Henrietta said. "We have work to do."

Together they heaved Mara's body up the cabin steps and out onto the deck, where Tanan rolled her inside a tarp. With an unceremonious splash, her body dropped overboard.

Henrietta checked her diamond watch. "I think enough time has passed for us to approach Monk's Cove unobserved," she said. "Take the boat close to the shore, Tanan. But take care. We don't want to alert them to our presence."

"We won't do that," said Tanan with a grin. "We are invisible."

The laptop winked on the table, showing Tanan's digital sketch of the yacht they were on. The color and contrast had been adjusted to the point where the sketch all but blended with the backlit screen.

Henrietta found that she was starting to regret the valerian root. Tanan would be dead in a matter of days, and here he was proving so useful.

"We must still use caution," she said. "Quickly now. We must be there when Emily opens Hollow Earth or we will not be able to enter and help my son."

The air on deck was cold. Henrietta tied an Hermès scarf around her head to protect her ears from the wind and admired the steel gray of the sky as Tanan piloted the boat along the small island's coast. As Monk's Cove came into view, Henrietta lifted the binoculars to her eyes again.

Em was on the cliff side with Sandie, Vaughn, and the deaf, fair-haired boy from the abbey whose name Henrietta did not know. They were wriggling into a hole, carrying something bulky. Henrietta adjusted the binoculars and squinted. A painting.

So that is how she will do it, she thought admiringly. *My granddaughter is even more powerful than I imagined.*

Hollow Earth was so close now, she could almost touch it.

"Soon," she said to herself. "Soon, *mon cheri,* we will take power from them all."

Distracted by her own arrogance, Henrietta failed to notice two figures in black climbing on board the boat behind her.

SEVENTY-TWO

It was a short drop to the rocky floor of the painted cavern where she and Matt had fought off Tanan's scaly demon over the summer. Em felt a frisson of fear at the memory. She turned on her flashlight and held it up to light the vast chamber.

Vaughn set the triptych on the ground, wiped his hands on his jacket, and whistled. "Look at this place," he said. "I can't believe I've never discovered this cave before."

"The drawings are over there," Em said, pointing to massive etchings on the far wall of the cavern.

"How long do you think they've been here?" signed Zach, looking at the images in wonder.

"Perhaps Albion and the early monks of Era Mina painted

them," Sandie replied. "They look like they predate *The Book of Beasts*. Are you ready, Em?"

Em felt support from Zach's mind to her own. She nodded.

"Right," said Vaughn. "I'm going to tie us together so we don't get separated, whatever happens."

Em clasped her hands together to stop them from trembling as Vaughn looped the rope around their waists. If she got this right, she would see Matt again. If she failed . . .

You won't fail.

How do you know, Zach?

I just know.

"Good to go," said Vaughn, tightening the last knot. "All right, Em. This is up to you now."

Sandie squeezed Em's hand, boosting her confidence. Keeping her eyes averted from the wounded Matt in the left-hand panel, Em focused her mind on the painted cave mouth.

Em felt the ground beneath her feet tremble. The etched beasts on the cave walls began to synchronize their pulsing to the beat of her own heart. The hellhound's four eyes snapped open, sending a shock wave bouncing around the walls of the chamber, and a low rumbling howl shook the ground under their feet, shooting up the wall in a wave of brilliant energy that burst suddenly from the snapping jaws of the beast, flashed across the cave, and hit the panel on the painting in an explosion of yellow light.

The hellhound thrashed from side to side as if it was trying to tear itself free. Em heard her mum gasp. She felt a tug on the rope at her waist.

In her imagination Em took control of the light. The paint on her triptych lifted off the panel in ribbons that wrapped around her feet. The ribbons moved up her legs and surrounded her entire body in a cyclone of bright colors. The gyre widened, the brilliance of the colors wrapping around Em's chest, forcing the breath from her lungs. She squeezed Zach's hand. He squeezed back.

Her feet lifted from the ground. Zach's fingers were slipping from her grip.

Em's ears began to pop. They were falling fast. The colors were brighter, the surging air stronger the deeper they plunged. Em clung to the fact that the rope around her waist was taut. The four of them were still connected.

Zach, can you hear me?

Yes!

She could hear roaring now. The beasts were near. She was doing this for Matt. She was—

Em landed on something soft with a grunt. The others fell beside her, gasping in shock.

"What a ride," Vaughn croaked. "Everyone okay?"

Sandie patted the ground curiously. "This is fur. Did we land on some kind of rug?"

Zach tapped urgently on Vaughn's shoulder. His hands spelled five shaky letters.

"BEAST."

Everyone scrambled off the humped, furry back they had landed on and pressed their backs to the wall. The sleeping beast's fur was tufted like a sheep's, but its bulk was closer to that of an elephant. Em could see neither a head nor a tail.

"What *is* that thing?" she gasped.

"No idea," said Vaughn.

"Maybe a Heffalump," signed Zach.

Em couldn't help herself. She giggled. "If this is a Heffalump, what does Piglet look like down here?"

"Whatever it is," said Sandie breathlessly, "I don't want to be here when it wakes up."

Zach wrinkled his nose. "This place smells worse than a cow shed."

Although it was dark, they didn't need to turn on their flashlights. The walls looked like they were covered in glowing green foil. The chamber was as wide as a gymnasium, and when Em looked up she could see swirling ink blots of color in the ceiling, as if she were looking up at an expressionist's canvas.

"I think it's some kind of antechamber," she said. Then she pointed to the other side of the cavern. "There's a tunnel, look."

Keeping their backs to the walls, the four of them followed Em to the tunnel's shadowy entrance.

SEVENTY-THREE

As they stepped into the glowing green tunnel, the noise hit them like a tidal wave. Roars and bellows, screeches and screams. The whole place vibrated with sound, blasting into them and through them and around them. The din was everywhere, feral and full of fury.

"We'll destroy our eardrums if we keep going forward in this," shouted Vaughn.

He pulled a sketch pad from one of his front pockets and swiftly sketched several sets of earplugs, which rolled from the sketch pad one pair at a time. Em caught hers and pushed them into her ears as far as she could. They helped—but only a little.

Zach's shocked expression caught Em's attention.

Can you hear the beasts screaming, Zach?

His response was hesitant. *I felt the same thing, the first time I saw your painting. I hope the beasts responsible are in cages.*

There was a curve in the tunnel up ahead. Rounding it, Em saw a bright line pulsing in the distance like a horizon at sunset.

The closer they got to the light, the wider and higher it became. When at last they reached it, it stood as wide as a door and as tall as Vaughn.

Zach's face was a picture of disgust. *It smells like a bear's den and the bear has died.*

It smells like boys' dirty laundry, you mean, Em replied.

Without thinking, she put her fingers against the curtain of light.

"Don't!" said Vaughn sharply, but he was too late.

As Em's fingertips touched the wall of light, she lit up like a Christmas tree. She was absorbed into the glowing curtain like water, disappearing in an instant.

SEVENTY-FOUR

Em found herself on a ledge, halfway down a colossal gorge of volcanic rock. Thanks to Vaughn's climbing rope, the others were still with her. The uneven ledge was barely wider than a bicycle lane and circumvented the gorge like a rocky catwalk. The geological architecture of the place reminded Em of the setting of a horror movie, the rocks forming castlelike turrets and needle-sharp spires.

Steadying herself on the rocky cliff behind her, Em looked up. The rock face was slick with lichens that shimmered with a silvery luster. Other parts of the gorge were thick with bright, multicolored moss. Odd-shaped trees sprouted sideways from the massive cliff walls, their roots coursing through the rocks like veins. The walls of the gorge stretched above them into blackness.

Em wasn't sure if it was a night sky or just an eternal darkness. The thought made her shiver. Zach took her hand.

As Vaughn untied the rope that connected them, Em allowed her gaze to drop. Everywhere there were beasts.

Hundreds of grottoes and chambers lined the gorge and were occupied by winged creatures of every imaginable size and shape, some perched, some flying, and all screaming and squawking. Decaying wraiths and devilish gargoyles wheeled through the gloom, trailing partially devoured carcasses and broken skeletal remains in their claws. Half-chewed beast heads lay skewered on some of the sharper needle-shaped rocks, dropped by the flying beasts overhead, while the flayed and stinking skins of beasts littered much of the ledge Em and the others were standing on.

The arches framing the grottoes were covered in reliefs of beasts and demons howling and writhing against the rock. Everywhere she looked, Em recognized a beast from a fable or a story. Everything seemed to bulge outward, threatening and grotesque and pulsing with life. The din was deafening, the earplugs about as useful as cotton wool. And the stink reminded Em of the putrid smells carried in the wind from a slaughterhouse.

At the center of each grotto—at least, those Em could see—was a wall of text, in a language she didn't recognize.

"Looks like ancient Gaelic," said Sandie, gazing at the text.

The bottom of the gorge was dimly visible, its colossal structure reminding Em of a Roman amphitheater with arched entrances to tunnels at various places around the periphery. The dirt floor was alive with so much overwhelming movement and chaos—beasts and bodies colliding, attacking, fighting in a hideous vortex of hunger and hate—that it was difficult for Em to comprehend exactly what she was looking at. It reminded her of a painting she had once seen at the Prado in Madrid with her mum: a dark, horrifying picture of hell in Hieronymus Bosch's *Garden of Earthly Delights*. Fear bubbled in her mind like lava.

Don't try to absorb it all. I can feel your panic rising.

Em returned the pressure of Zach's hand, trying to calm herself.

The swoop above their heads was almost soundless.

"Move!" Sandie yelled.

Em gasped. Vaughn swore. They all ducked as a griffin the size of a small plane swooped out of nowhere at them. Em stumbled, knocking backward into Zach—who lost his footing and tumbled over the edge.

"ZACH!" Em screamed. She would go mad if she lost Zach as well as her brother . . .

Vaughn dived after Zach, grabbing his hand just in time, and yanked him back up onto the ledge. They both rolled back against the rock wall, panting hard. Em felt dizzy with relief.

The griffin cut a tight circle and came back at them, its great eyes as green and brilliant as emeralds. Its breath felt like a hot wind on their skin as its wing tips almost swept them from the ledge. It swooped straight up into the darkness again, then dived into the abyss, snatching up a creature that looked like a cross between a hippo and a tiger. As the griffin tore its prey in half with its paws, half of its bloody carcass dropped again to the ground, where it was instantly set upon.

The griffin banked again, gliding high and lazy, then dropped back toward the ledge, its wings tucked close to its thick golden haunches and its ferocious gaze intense.

It was coming for them next.

SEVENTY-FIVE

Anyone know anything useful about griffins?" screamed Sandie, her back pressed against the rock as the beast approached at breakneck speed.

"I'm thinking . . ." Em stammered.

"Think faster!"

Vaughn pulled his sketch pad from his jacket pocket, but the blast of wind from the Griffin's wings blew it from his hand and sent it spinning several meters along the ledge. Zach broke away from the wall and ran along the narrow rocky path to retrieve it.

"No!" yelled Em. *Zach, the griffin will get you! Stay back against the wall!*

Vaughn launched himself at Zach, bringing him to the ground as the griffin swept overhead, its sharp-edged wing slicing the front of Sandie's jacket and its heavy lion's tail thrashing across Vaughn's back.

"We can't stay on this ledge for much longer," said Sandie as Vaughn and Zach struggled to their feet, Zach clutching the sketchbook. "How are we supposed to fight a griffin?"

"Griffins are guardians of treasure," blurted Em, suddenly remembering. She felt in her pockets for a pencil. "If I draw some, we might distract its attention."

"Do it," said Vaughn. "Fast."

Em pulled the sketch pad from Zach's hands and scribbled, fingers flying.

In a burst of yellow light, a treasure chest overflowing with gold and silver doubloons appeared on the ledge.

At once the griffin swooped down from a great height, its eyes blazing, and landed on the ledge, a few paces from Em and Zach, snapping its hooked beak. Then it pounced.

Sandie screamed, reaching for Zach and Em.

"Wait," Vaughn said, pulling her back. "Look!"

The griffin had climbed on top of the treasure chest and was wrapping its wings protectively over the doubloons, knocking a cache of them over the ledge into the chaos below.

"Where now?" said Sandie.

Em gazed down into the abyss. The arches around the periphery of the amphitheater-like pit looked familiar.

"I painted one of those in the left-hand panel of my triptych," she said, pointing at the arches. "If my painting is right, Matt—

maybe Jeannie, too—will come through one of those tunnels. They'll run right into that hell. We have to be there for them."

"But how do we get down there?" said Sandie helplessly. "We must be at least a hundred meters up! And how do we survive when we reach the ground?"

"One thing at a time," said Vaughn. He gazed over the edge of the ledge, assessing the rock face. "The gorge walls are rough; there are plenty of foot- and handholds. If we start now, we can be at the bottom in half an hour."

Zach raised his hand. "I don't think we have that kind of time," he signed. "Something monstrous is coming. And it's bringing Matt and Jeannie with it."

Em sensed something much worse than fear from Zach. She felt terror.

"Are they okay?" she signed back at once. "How do you know they're with this thing?"

Zach pressed a shaky hand to his chest. *I feel it here.*

Sandie was staring over the edge. "I think the beasts agree with Zach," she said.

The pit was emptying in a violent stampede. Beast galloped, grunted, and gored their way into the various tunnels, leaving a tide of blood in their wake that flowed into the crevices and crannies in the ground. Em watched a yale—an odd bovinelike beast that could have been an ancestor to a Highland cow—skewer a wild boar with one of its armlike horns and toss it into the air in a desperate bid for freedom. The air swarmed with cockatrices, manticores, and firebirds; gargoyles and rocs fought with orcs and Owlmen, trolls with Valkyries. . . . Everything was desperate to leave.

To put as much space as possible between themselves and whatever was coming.

SEVENTY-SIX

We need a fast way down," said Vaughn as the stampede in the air and on the ground reached a crescendo. "Think!"

"A giant airbag?" said Sandie. "The kind of thing you see stuntmen jump onto from tall buildings?"

"Too unpredictable," said Vaughn. "What if one of us lands badly and breaks a leg, or worse? What if one of these flying beasts swoops past in midjump and picks us off as lunch?"

Em stared up at the spires and towers, the nooks and crannies of the gruesome gorge. They couldn't stay up here.

Em suddenly remembered the construction site at one of the old mansions in Kensington Gardens.

"A slide!" she said. "Like those long tubes they use on demolition sites to get rid of rubbish and debris."

A million sets of eyes stared down at the four of them, the beasts of the air watching them like they were field mice. Em grabbed Vaughn's sketch pad and animated a tubular slide, fusing it onto a thick root jutting out of the rock face. The tube extended like a telescope, one section expanding from another in lightning cracks of light, until the last tube hit the distant ground with a hollow clang.

"Sandie, you go first down the chute," said Vaughn, sketching at the same time as Em. "As soon as you get to the bottom, clear out of the way and get inside that for safety."

He pointed to a cage on wheels that he'd animated around the airy cushion at the bottom of Em's slide.

Sandie wriggled into the tube first. She disappeared almost at once. Em followed.

The ride was breathtakingly fast. Em rocketed in a wide spiral down to the bottom of the gorge, slewing from side to side, the tube walls a blur. She emerged with a gasp in the cage Vaughn had created, bouncing next to her mother on the cushion. Zach and then Vaughn exploded from the tube behind her, almost cart-wheeling into the bars of the cage.

Way above them, a dragon shot out of a crevice, spewing fire at the very spot where they had been standing moments earlier. The edge of the tube caught on fire.

"What the . . ."

Vaughn gave an exclamation as the paper in his hand burst into flames. They could only watch as the tube, their protective cage, and the drawing flared away to nothing, leaving them alone and defenseless on the rocky, bloodied ground.

The ground trembled. An overwhelming stench of rotting flesh and sewage gusted down the nearest tunnel, causing Em, Zach, Sandie, and Vaughn to gag and cover their noses.

Through the gloom, a hulking shape was moving slowly toward them.

We have got to move from here fast, Zach. Something really bad is coming. I can feel it.

And then Em heard a familiar shout, deep in her mind.

OH . . . MY . . . GOD . . . EM! Am I hallucinating, or is that your obnoxious voice I can hear?

SEVENTY-SEVEN

M ATT!" Em screamed out loud. "Mum, Zach, Vaughn—I can hear Matt!"

Sandie's face flooded with color as her eyes darted in every direction, landing on the entrance to the foul-smelling tunnel.

Matt was still yelling in Em's head, making it impossible to hear herself think. But it was the best distraction ever. Despite their circumstances, she found herself laughing and crying at the same time.

Tears were spilling down Em's cheeks. She threw herself into Zach's arms and danced a jig with him. *We came to find you, Matt. We opened this place to come and find you! Are you okay?*

"Is Mattie hurt?" Sandie begged. "Tell me, Em, is he okay?"

At the thought of Matt wounded as she had painted him

in her triptych, Em found that he was gone from her mind. She grasped blindly, trying to find him again.

Matt! Can you hear me?

Nothing.

Zach saw and felt Em's panic rising. *What's wrong? Have you lost him?*

Em nodded in anguish.

The grendel lurched out of the tunnel in front of her.

At first Em thought its body was made of soft, wet clay. Then she saw it more clearly. Layers and layers of mud were peppered with hundreds of pulsing holes, like empty eyes blinking in the darkness. The creature oozed through the tunnel into the great pit in front of them, red eyes flaming, the stench of decay hanging over it like a shroud. Em stumbled back in disgust and horror.

Matt! Can you hear me?

Had they found Matt, just to lose him again?

Sandie yelped as she crunched across a nest of bones that was sinking into the ground. Vaughn reached over and lifted her off.

"Pick a tunnel," said Vaughn as the grendel advanced, inhaling the air around it, creating a death draft that sucked the bones on the ground toward it with a hideous clattering sound. "We have to get out of here."

But every tunnel Em could see was full of countless monsters, stopping and turning and shifting forward in an ugly kind of unison. Their fear and stench was overwhelming. Suffocating.

Em felt her mother's hand grip her own. "We need weapons."

"A tank?" signed Zach. "We could use it to charge our way into one of those tunnels."

The watching, waiting creatures of Hollow Earth moved more quickly than Em would have dreamed possible. In moments they were utterly surrounded: the grendel before them, the nightmarish beasts behind.

Trapped.

Em wondered wildly if the beasts had tricked them, cleared the pit to lure them from the ledge to their doom. It was as if they were thinking as one.

Where was her brother? Why couldn't she hear him anymore? *Matt! Matt!*

An enormous serpent creature with the crested head and spindly legs of a cockerel bounded toward Sandie. Vaughn was drawing, but he wasn't fast enough. The beast whipped its thick snake's tail and knocked the pad from his hand.

"It's a basilisk, Mum," screamed Em in blind panic. "Don't let it breathe on you! Its breath is poisonous! Vaughn, draw us weapons—anything! *Hurry!*"

Vaughn scrambled for his pad. In seconds they were armed with glittering, sparking swords. As the basilisk lunged at Sandie, she dropped onto her knees, ducked beneath its toxic beak, and slid her sword into its feathered breast.

The basilisk gave an unearthly scream. Sandie only just rolled out of the way before the monster collapsed to the ground. The grendel was across the pit in a blur, sucking out the basilisk's heart and stripping its feathers and flesh. It lifted its enormous apelike head and bayed, bringing more creatures out of the tunnels, darkening the air above and the ground below with their writhing, fluttering, flexing bodies.

Em was filled with awe at the sight of her mother, dripping sword in hand, like the warriors Em loved to draw. The sight filled her with resolve. If her mother could be brave, she could too. The fear of this place wouldn't defeat her.

Em ran to her mum's side, ready for whatever horror was coming.

And then Matt and Jeannie stumbled out of the shadows.

SEVENTY-EIGHT

Matt and Jeannie were holding each other upright. Jeannie was still dressed in her orange safety vest, although it was tattered and torn at one shoulder. She and Matt were both limping. Matt was wounded, just as Em had painted him. But thankfully, the bone quill was clutched in his hand and no longer deep in his flesh.

Em grinned at her brother. *You took your time.*

Matt's face blazed with relief and delight. *I'm happy to see you, Em, but maybe we can do this whole reunion thing when we get out of this hellhole?*

Sandie ran over to Matt, ignoring the host of slithering serpents and flying beasts around them, and pulled him into a fierce mother's hug. Then she turned and tearfully embraced Jeannie.

"Thank you," she said.

"Ach, lass," said Jeannie. "It was nothing."

"I hate to break up the reunion," said Vaughn, "but we have a problem."

In the moments that Sandie had taken to reach Matt, Zach and Em had gotten cut off from the others. Now they were staring down a drake: a two-legged, horned dragon with a crocodile's tail. The beast was spitting green fireballs at them that exploded into toxic slime at their feet.

Zach touched Em, pulling her gaze from Matt. *When I give the signal, Em.*

He thrust his sword at the beast's head, jabbing its wide nose. The drake roared with rage. A ball of green flame landed at Zach's feet; another seared the shoulder of his jacket, but he kept jabbing.

Now!

Em pictured her mother killing the basilisk. She jumped into the air, flashing her sword, driving its shining blade through the monster's thick scales and into the drake's back. As it turned its horned head in agony to spit fire at her, Zach thrust his sword deep into its leathery neck, earning a spray of green, smelly blood that gushed all over him. He choked, covering his nose.

Whoa . . . this stuff stinks like pee.

Em animated a lavender-scented towel. Hardly pausing to thrust it into Zach's gunky hands, she raced across the cavern and threw herself into Matt's arms.

"Ow!" Matt mumbled, squeezing her weakly. "Injured man here, okay?"

Em jumped back as she remembered his wound. To her horror, her brother wobbled and fell to the ground.

"He'll be okay, lass," said Jeannie, looking at Sandie and embracing Em and Zach together as Sandie and Vaughn gently lifted Matt back onto his feet, "but we need to get him out of here. He's lost a fair amount of blood."

Vaughn moved to the entrance of the tunnel, staring out into the pit, where things were not looking good for them.

Sandie studied the snarling, snapping beasts surrounding them. "Guys, we really need to get out of here."

Vaughn looked at Jeannie and squeezed her arm. "Any ideas?" he said.

Jeannie smiled.

SEVENTY-NINE

Setting her hands flat on the creviced cliff wall, Jeannie closed her eyes to summon their salvation.

At first only the area of rock directly under her palms pulsed, outlining her hands with a pale green light. But then the pulsing rhythm spread out across the wall, shooting light in every direction, illuminating the colossal cavern with veins of brilliance that throbbed with the steady cadence of a heartbeat.

"We need more than pretty lights," Vaughn said. "Are you sure this will work?"

"You never did really listen to my stories, did you, son?" Jeannie sighed. "He'll come. Have a wee bit of faith."

"We need to get Matt on a stretcher," said Em, holding her semiconscious brother's hand. "Mum, can you draw one?"

Sandie animated a simple length of canvas with two poles through loops on each side. Once Matt was settled, they waited, huddled together for warmth and comfort, keeping one eye on the prowling beasts and one on Jeannie's light show as it made the great, gloomy cavern shine as brightly as a fairground ride.

A golden glow shimmered in the air above them, right in the center of the cavernous space. Silent now, the beasts began to part like the Red Sea. Not one creature bayed, howled, lunged, or growled. Even the grendel fell silent.

Albion walked among them, dressed from head to toe in a fur cloak and white gown, the familiar silver helix spinning on his breastplate. His crown of antlers was gold and shining as bright as a hundred torches.

Gripping his carved wooden scepter, he stopped in front of Jeannie and bowed. He turned to Em and did the same. Em bobbed an awkward curtsy in return.

"Thank you," Albion said, in a voice that sounded as if it hadn't been used in centuries. "For listening to your imagination."

Then with his heavy fur cloak brushing the ground, Albion held his scepter aloft. The golden light from his antler crown expanded, filling the space with even more brightness. And a beam shone from the peryton set in the top of the scepter to a dark cave mouth far up on the gorge walls, farther even than the ledge where they had first entered Albion's kingdom.

"There's our way home," said Em.

And she pointed to where the white peryton was waiting for them at the mouth of the cave.

EIGHTY

When Simon spotted a rolled blue tarp dropping from nowhere into the choppy bay, he knew they had found Henrietta de Court.

With Renard using all his abilities to cloak their presence, they had successfully crept up onto the sleek blue cruiser. It had been almost impossible to see. If it hadn't been for the splash, they would never have found it.

Henrietta stood on the deck, her hair tied back in a scarf and her binoculars trained on Era Mina. While Renard held the small abbey boat steady, well out of Henrietta's sight line, Simon climbed stealthily over the side, slipping a syringe from its leather wrap. Henrietta didn't look around.

Tanan was piloting the craft from the top deck, wind in his

dark hair and aviators on his nose. Simon climbed up the side of the boat and dropped lightly behind him.

Tanan's reactions weren't fast enough. Simon plunged the tranquilizer deep into his thigh, catching him as he slumped to the ground.

Simon set the cruiser to autopilot, after tying Tanan's hands firmly behind his back. He wouldn't wake up for a while, but there was no point in taking chances. Then he climbed back down to the deck.

Henrietta was still watching the small island, crooning softly to herself as she adjusted the binoculars. At the swift plunge of Simon's needle, she fell into his arms. In a matter of moments, she was trussed up like a turkey and left on the deck to wake up in her own good time.

"I have them both," Simon said, returning to the cabin. "Renard?"

Renard was gazing at the tapestry, which he had unfurled inside the cabin.

"Look at this, Simon," he said.

The great tapestry showed Malcolm as a knight with wings on his shoulder plates and a swirling helix on his breastplate, leading an army of skeletal black knights. As they watched, the threads were brightening, burning, restitching themselves into a fresh design, a different pattern, a new story.

Renard turned at last to the open laptop. "Clever," he said, pointing at the cloaked image on the screen. "Let's add a little contrast, shall we?"

At the press of a button, the cruiser emerged in fully defined detail.

"Let's sail this little beauty over to Monk's Cove," said Simon, stroking the gleaming interior. "It would be a shame to get rid of it too soon."

"A fine idea," Renard agreed, settling himself in one of the comfortable chairs belowdecks. "You can take the helm."

Simon was already ascending the polished wooden steps two at a time to the wheel above. Across on the island, he could see a bright flash of light from deep within the hillside.

Swiping the aviators from the unconscious Tanan, Simon set them on his own nose.

It was time to bring the family home in style.

EIGHTY-ONE

They took Matt and Jeannie directly to the hospital in Largs. The cruiser made short work of the crossing, and as Largs came into view, Matt started stirring and making lame jokes. He was so glad to be home, he thought he might burst.

Once he'd heard about the events that occurred while he was gone, he pointed at the great carpet of fabric on the floor.

"Is that the tapestry that Henrietta stole from the Council, Grandpa?" he asked.

"Stunning, isn't it?" said Renard. He helped Matt up to take a closer look. "What do you think?"

What Matt saw made him very happy. Instead of Malcolm riding on the black peryton with a crush of bodies at his feet, the tapestry that would be returned to the Council chambers at the

Royal Academy now depicted a spiky-haired girl in Viking armor standing on a jagged rock, firing arrows at a line of skeletal half-faced knights on a beach. In the foreground, a tall, leather-clad knight looking a lot like Solon was riding on a majestic white peryton, its mighty wings folded against its haunches, a line of villagers behind him in triumphant procession, making their way toward the monastery.

GLOSSARY

The abbey: The abbey on Auchinmurn Isle started its life as a fortress, then become a monastery housing a community of monks in the early Middle Ages, developing into a modern home and place of learning in the twenty-first century. Through time, wars, and strife, the buildings and their continuous line of owners have held the islands of Auchinmurn and Era Mina together and kept their secrets safe.

Animare (s and pl): A person who can bring pictures to life by drawing. The fact of their existence is known to only a few, but there are those who wish to use the powers of Animare for their own evil gain. For this reason, Animare live by the Five Rules:

- They mustn't animate in public.
- They must always be in control of their imaginations.
- If they endanger the secret of their existence, they can be "bound" (see below).

- They are forbidden from having children with Guardians (see below), as this can result in dangerous hybrids with an unpredictable mix of powers.
- Children cannot be bound.

Binding: Binding is a kind of suspended animation. Animare are bound into a work of art as a last resort when they lose control of their powers or endanger the secret of their existence. Binding an Animare can be authorized only by the Council of Guardians, and can take place only when both a Guardian and a second Animare are present.

There are five secure vaults all over the world containing bound paintings. One lies at the abbey on Auchinmurn Isle.

Council of Guardians: A body of Guardians who enforce the Five Rules for Animare. Council members do not always agree about how Animare should be guided. When hybrid children are created, for example, some Guardians believe that their talents should be nurtured, while others believe that binding (see above) is the only safe course of action.

Guardian: A Guardian helps to keep an Animare's powers and emotions under control. Each Animare is allocated a specific Guardian. A Guardian's ability to influence an Animare's way of thinking is known as "inspiriting." Guardians can use this power on other people as well.

Hollow Earth: The supernatural place where all monsters, demons, devils, and creatures from the dangerous, magical past have been trapped by the medieval monks of the Order of Era Mina (see below).

The Hollow Earth Society: Founded by Duncan Fox in 1848, the original Hollow Earth Society was designed to prevent the world from knowing about the monsters and imagined creatures locked away in Hollow Earth. The reformed Hollow Earth Society has a very different outlook: to retrieve the monsters, control them, and unleash them on the world.

The Order of Era Mina: The monks in medieval Auchinmurn belonged to the Order of Era Mina, which had a particular mission: locking away the monsters of the superstitious past by drawing them into a bestiary called the *Book of Beasts*, thereby reinventing the world as a modern place of enlightenment and learning.

ACKNOWLEDGMENTS

From the start, we knew how this trilogy would begin and how it would end, but we'd never have made it from there to here without help. To our extraordinary UK editor, Lucy Courtenay, who knows Matt and Em as well as we do, the biggest thank you . . . imaginable.

Three big cheers to Fiona Simpson and all at Aladdin Books for coming along on this journey, and fist bumps to Laura Palmer and the folks at Head of Zeus who will travel to the future with us. And "yay" to our agents, Georgina Capel and Gavin Barker.

To our spouses, Kevin Casey and Scott Gill, our parents, Marion and John Barrowman, and the rest of our clan (especially Turner & Hannah; Clare, Casey & Finn), without you all we'd be truly lost. Thank you for making this literary journey much less bumpy and for being the rest stops whenever we needed one—

CB: Which was a lot.
JB: You can't have the last words.
CB: Yes, I can.
~~JB: No, you can't.~~

Carole and John
2015